MANHATTAN MELTDOWN

GUERNICA WORLD EDITIONS 40

MANHATTAN MELTDOWN

Frank Lentricchia

GUERNICA
World
EDITIONS

TORONTO—CHICAGO—BUFFALO—LANCASTER (U.K.)
2021

Michael Mirolla, editor
Cover design: Allen Jomoc Jr.
Interior layout: Jill Ronsley, suneditwrite.com
Guernica Editions Inc.
287 Templemead Drive, Hamilton (ON), Canada L8W 2W4
2250 Military Road, Tonawanda, N.Y. 14150-6000 U.S.A.
www.guernicaeditions.com

Distributors:
Independent Publishers Group (IPG)
600 North Pulaski Road, Chicago IL 60624
University of Toronto Press Distribution (UTP)
5201 Dufferin Street, Toronto (ON), Canada M3H 5T8
Gazelle Book Services, White Cross Mills
High Town, Lancaster LA1 4XS U.K.

First edition.

Legal Deposit—Third Quarter
Library of Congress Catalog Card Number: 2021933676
Library and Archives Canada Cataloguing in Publication
Title: Manhattan meltdown / Frank Lentricchia.
Names: Lentricchia, Frank, author.
Series: Guernica world editions ; 40.
Description: Series statement: Guernica world editions ; 40 Identifiers:
Canadiana (print) 20210142952 | Canadiana (ebook) 20210142995 |
ISBN 9781771836753 (softcover) | ISBN 9781771836760 (EPUB) |
ISBN 9781771836777 (Kindle)
Classification: LCC PS3562.E57 M36 2021 | DDC 813/.54—dc23

This one is for:

Samuele Pardini
Tara Pardini
and
Dante Pardini

Unendowed with wealth or pity,
Little birds with scarlet legs,
Sitting on their speckled eggs,
Eye each flu-infected city.

Altogether elsewhere, vast
Herds of reindeer move across
Miles and miles of golden moss,
Silently and very fast.

—W.H. Auden, "The Fall of Rome"

Early March, 2020

New York City

1

The big black man reaches over and grips the hand of the big white man. The big white man closes his eyes and trembles. The big black man lowers the shade. The big black man leans into the big white man. He whispers, "I'm here."

Directly in front of the big black man a boy-child whines, "Mommy, I don't want to go in the water." Earbuds affixed, Mommy does not hear. She's rockin' her life away.

Over the intercom: "Good morning, folks, and good grief. Flight attendants, cross-check and prepare for landing." He switches off.

Syracuse to New York's La Guardia in a small Delta jet, frequently and violently buffeted.

The big white man speaks through his constricted throat, "Flight attendants? Plural? There's only one. What's cross-check, Robby? Tell me if you know." The big black man responds, "No one knows." The big black man leans in again. He whispers, "Try not to breathe so fast."

The pilot: "Folks, should you be curious, those rough waters below, not that far below," chuckling, "that's Flushing Bay. Enjoy the view, if you dare." He switches off. Immediately switches back on: "My First Officer, she's mine, yes, the incomparable know-it-all Gina Rendonello, she informs me that it's Bowery Bay, not Flushing." He croons, "Oh Geeeeena! Flushing, Bowery, let's call the whole thing off. Enjoy your stay in the New York area, or wherever your final destination may be." Chuckling again. "Final destination in any sense." Before he switches off, a female voice from the cockpit: "The whole thing was never on. Asshole."

Silence in the cabin. Who are these people in the cockpit—inaccessible behind the post 9/11 fortified door?

Forty-five minutes of relentless turbulence, featuring five sudden stomach-in-your throat plunges, for God only knows how many feet toward annihilation. Seat belt sign never turned off. The flight attendant buckled in the entire time, checking his cell, re-applying his make-up, while the stiff drink that so many require—including four recovering alcoholics—is never delivered. Staring at his phone, the flight attendant cross-checks, in his imagination.

The child lunges toward Mommy, but cannot move. Too tightly buckled in. He touches Mommy's oblivious arm.

Twelve seconds from landing the plane pulls up steeply just short of vertical ascent. Screaming in the cabin—except for the big black man, the absent mother, and her small child, who loves scary carnival rides. They circle for 17 minutes and approach from the other side of La Guardia. Over land, not water.

The bi-racial—what shall they be called? Couple? Why not? They are seated mid-way back in the cabin. They are not racially-enlightened gay men. They are friends, without conscious homoerotic urges toward one another, or anyone else, who had never hesitated (much less feared) to show affection, each to each. The arm around the shoulder. The hug. No. Not the pat, not the slap on the ass, gestures reserved for elite athletes on the fields of play. Once, and only once, at the big black man's retirement party, the big white man launched the ass slap, but halted, hand frozen inches from its targeted black butt, as he smiled.

The two pals have come to New York City not to see the "sights," or to attend brutally expensive and less than mediocre Broadway theater, or for the incomparable museums, or to walk through the heart-stopping canyons of Lower Broadway. Many years ago, they had come for just such reasons. The two pals from childhood have come this time to New York City with a secret. Each with a purpose unknown to the other.

At the gate, the black man says, "Let's stay seated. Let's be the last ones off. Because I have a question for the cockpit. I want some clarifying f-ing dialogue." He says f-ing, not the actual word. In the last phase of his life he seeks to purge his long-practiced foulmouth. Because he needs to become a different man. Because he's sick of himself. Sick of the sound of his voice echoing endlessly in his memory. How shall he rid himself of memory? He's simmering. He's been simmering for decades.

The white man says, too loudly, as those with compromised hearing tend to do, "I succeeded. I wonder if anyone else failed to do so."

"You succeeded in what?" says the black man. Whose hearing is not yet, but will soon be compromised, if he manages to eke out a few more years. Says the white man, "I held my bowels." The black man grins and says, "Welcome back from the f-ing abyss."

The black man is Antonio Robinson ("Robby"), former All-American running back at Syracuse University, retired Utica, New York Chief of Police, divorced, with estranged children who despise him, thanks to his ex-wife's successful years-long campaign of vilification. He must cease to care about his kids. Good luck with that, Chief Robinson.

The white man is Eliot Conte ("El"). A man eviscerated by life-long worries over anything and everything. He's a former Private Investigator, part time professor of American literature at Utica College, and author of a recently published book on Herman Melville, the subject of which is the recurring appearance of a single word and its synonyms in *Moby-Dick*. The word is *appalling*.

Six weeks ago Conte survived six hours of open-heart surgery, under the knife of the morbid comedian Dr. Harry Gallatin. Conte is married (happily enough—etcetera) and has courageously, or insanely, at his age, a six-year-old daughter. The two friends turned 74 on the same day four months ago. If you saw them walking toward you, you would cross quickly to the other side of the street. Because you would find them appalling.

At the gate, Captain J.W. Kidd stands in the open doorway of the flight deck. Or cockpit, if you will. Like all commercial pilots, the Captain was instructed to say over the intercom "flight deck" rather than "cockpit," the latter to be avoided for its vulgar con-notation. Captain J.W. Kidd never failed to honor protocol, but in his mind each time he said "flight deck" he thought "cockpit." Because "cockpit" was the proper home for a man proud of his exploits, however lightning-quick. The fabled Speedy Gonzalez, fastest dick in the West, has nothing on the Captain, who is tanned year round, extremely fit, 5'7" in shoes. Some would consider him, as he does himself, quite handsome. See him now wishing all good things for each of the exiting passengers, one with a badly torn shirt, another without shoes, a few others wrapped in the faint odor of sewage. He's warning them to "Watch your step as you de-plane." The flight attendant has departed before the passen-gers, at Captain Kidd's kind insistence. Captain Kidd considers himself generous, and often is.

First Officer Gina Rendonello sits at her station, back to the Captain and the shattered de-planers, as she writes on a form at-tached to a clipboard. She's tall for a female of Italian-American extraction. A six-footer in bare feet and head-turningly attractive. (Female beauty at that altitude? Goddess territory.) She does not regard herself as attractive, who suffers periodic outbreaks of acne, which she does not hide under makeup thickly applied. She has no idea why anyone would find her attractive, with or without the acne.

What was it that caused men—the eligible, as they are called—heterosexual, not in failing health in their 70s, intelligent, known as "cultured," employed and even with a sense of humor— to fear her? The height of Gina Rendonello? More likely than you'd think. Her self-assurance? Directness of speech and manner, so easily misread as toughness? She's had, believes she'll always have, a life romantically barren.

The Captain watches two last passengers, two men with stiff lower backs struggling to rise and extract their luggage from the overhead bin. The black man succeeding, the white man failing. The black man doing it for the white man. They move forward, the black man leading the way. Partially bald, he has refused the shaved dome fashion inspired by a basketball icon—a look now imitated by white men with severely challenged hair lines. Thinks the Captain, *Fat black dude hasn't gone for the look. Blacks shave it off, they look terrific. White guys? We become serial killers.*

The Captain at 36 is losing it on top: an expanding bald spot in the back of the head, checked daily in the bathroom mirror with a hand-held mirror properly angled for the chilling view. Viewed daily, he knows, by all who walk behind him. What remains is fetching—totally sexy, he feels—from a certain angle in the hand-held mirror. He envisions it all fleeing him. On the floor, in the sink, in the shower, in his mouth (of nonerotic provenance), on his clothes, on his pillow and plucked, with care, from the keyboard of his laptop and pulled, a long one, from his oatmeal. All departed by his mid-forties. He knows the terror of his family history.

The Captain has persuaded his primary-care physician to write a prescription for a hair-restoring and libido-crushing drug. He's been on it for 2 weeks. He believes that by his mid-forties a new drug will have been concocted. The new wonder drug to be taken daily with the hair-restoring libido-crusher and guaranteed to restore his manhood. The Captain sees himself at 45 bushy-haired as never before, and flaccid no more.

The white man shuffles two steps behind his black friend. Only the top of the white man's head of thick, wavy hair is visible to Captain Kidd, whose view is dominated by the overweight black man looming with every limping step. The black man comes ever closer to the Captain, formerly 6'2 ½," 200 pounds of coiled muscle, now 6'1", 245 pounds. The shrinkage of the golden years, the spreading feet of the golden years. A black block of limping flesh. But carrying it still, even with the limp—still flashing a trace of his former athletic grace, this All-American who never played on NFL Sundays because he blew out his knee in his last game, senior year, never again to bolt, slant and slash with the crazy capacity of a human hummingbird, once capable of 90 degree turns without loss of speed. And now they enter the wide area of the galley and exit door and Captain Kidd sees at last the whole of Eliot Conte, once 6'5", 235, now 6'3 ½," 170.

The narrow-shouldered Kidd, in shoes with soles and heels thicker than normal—a touch over 5'5" in bare feet—confronted now by two impressively broad-shouldered men. Kidd lifts his gaze to the old dudes. He is riveted by the gaunt white man's heart-diseased figure: Bones. Bones prominent in the shoulder. Jutting collar bones. Hip bones. Bones in the face, jutting cheek bones. A comical contrast, thinks the Captain, to this roly-poly black dude, this benign black dude, whose friend, son of Frankenstein's monster—could his Mommy ever love him? So thinks Kidd, this bristling bantam, who says, "Don't de-plane, don't even think about it, young fellas. I'll summon the wheelchairs."

The Captain feels First Officer Rendonello standing close behind as he inhales her fragrance (not perfume or cologne-produced) in the open narrow doorway of the cockpit. He does not step aside to let her through. From over his shoulder she nods and winks at the two big men standing before the Captain, a few feet away. These big men, these 74 year olds, feel themselves levitated far over their years by this winking beauty. Seventy-four? What is seventy-four? She winked, did she not? What, for that matter, is ninety-four, if they wink? She nodded, did she not? She smiled. Life is suddenly good after this flight through hell. Robinson winks in response. Conte nods and smiles his signature small smile—the once irresistible small smile.

Our Captain, who does not have eyes in the back of his head, situated in the expanding bald spot, assumes that the big men are smiling and winking at him. What are they? A pair of queens? Old queers gone to seed, coming on to him? Wouldn't be the first time, not by a long shot. Always the old ones. Or are they saying in their queerish style that they're grateful for my understanding and look forward to the arrival of the wheelchairs to take them through the zoo of the departure lounge, where I face the so-called support dogs that never fail to snarl at me? Especially the small ones. Why me? They sense a cold cat person, which is what

I am, though I'd never have one with odors of the litter box just off the kitchen.

J.W. Kidd pulls out his cell phone and says, "I'll have the chairs in a jiff—take a seat there in the first row. Take the load off, why don't you?"

Robinson says, "Put that f-ing thing away."

Conte says, with a growl, "I don't remember you, but I know we were once very close."

The two big men are expressionless. Rendonello grins.

J.W. Kidd in a thickened voice says, "It's really not a problem to make the call… the chairs… Why not take the load off…"

Elbowing her way out of the cockpit Rendonello says, "All of a sudden deaf, Jon Wilber? You heard the man."

Robinson says, "I bet my house it's John without the 'h'. Am I right, Cap?"

Conte says, "Wilber."

J.W. says, "Don't call me that. Don't call me Wilber."

Conte says, "Wilber, are you trying to control my—what's the word, Robby?"

Robinson says, "Tongue."

J.W. says, "De-plane now before I alert security."

Robinson says, "De-plane? What the f- kind of word is that? You wake up in the morning, what happens? You de-bed?"

Rendonello says, "Fasten your seat belt, J.W., sit back, relax, and enjoy the flight."

Conte says, "You see yourself shrinking. You are outside yourself, looking at yourself getting smaller. Your isolation becomes absolute."

Robinson says, as he and Conte take a step forward, "You pulled up at the last second. You owed us all a reason. You scared the s— out of us. Why? I want an answer. You arrogant little b—."

The Captain pivots and retreats into the cockpit, locking the door behind him.

* * *

The tall threesome—Robinson, Conte, Rendonello—move silently through the gray light of the empty bridge connecting plane and terminal, while two await them—two backlit, darkly clad in uniforms, at the threshold of the brightly lit terminal. Guns and Billy Clubs. Blocking the entrance. Behind the two uniforms, in civilian clothes, a woman of indeterminate race, holding close to her side, leashed, an unneutered big black dog, male, of indeterminate breed, on whose harness these words: DO NOT PET. The big black dog is wagging his tail. The connecting bridge is not wide enough to accommodate three big people abreast, pulling luggage. Robinson leads, with Conte behind and Rendonello third. She is mostly obscured by the two big men.

The threesome stops close, but not too close to the foursome comprised of the two security guards, the woman of the black dog, and the big black dog himself, wagging his tail and whimpering. The woman of the dog shifts her weight to the balls of her feet. She leans in toward the threesome. The dog sits.

Rendonello from behind Robinson and Conte shouts, "Blackie!"

One of the guards, a black female, shouts in response, "You racist cunt!"

The handler of the undisciplined bomb-and-drug-sniffer dog shouts, "You! Gina! What have you done to Captain Kidd?"

The dog called Blackie rolls over. (Because he's a good boy.) Excited penis on view. Gina steps around the armed guards and rubs so-called Blackie's underside.

The handler says, "Gina, you gave Jackie a problem. It's Jackie's problem—Jackie, Gina, not Blackie. Jackie. I don't want to think about his future. Do you care? You made him totally worthless for scoping luggage. He seeks affection, belly rubs and head scratching in the security queue, instead of contraband, thanks to what you started five weeks ago. You need a dog, Gina? You set him up for a special visit to the veterinarian. Follow me? The needle, Gina. The big sleep. The happy hunting ground of belly rubs."

The other security guard, the rotund one, apparently Caucasian, says, "We received a severe complaint from Captain Kidd. We're going downtown for questioning. Downtown Queens, if you want to know. Not Manhattan. To a precinct without Midtown glamour."

At which point Gina says, "What's the problem? The black guy is my uncle. The other is my fiancé."

At which point the black guard, La Tessica, says to her partner, "Julius, she's mocking us. She's in extreme contempt."

At which point, the handler, who calls herself Angie, says, "You two geniuses have any idea who she is? Didn't think so. Gina Rendonello. Rendonello ring any bells? Didn't think so. In this phony economy you appreciate your jobs? The health benefits? The guns and clubs? She just got off a Delta jet. You know this. You know Big Frank, as he is known in the industry? The envy of the industry? Big Frank rings no bells? Big Freakin' Frank Rendonello, CEO of Delta? I'm trying to put something into your thick skulls."

At which point Julius says, "We're just…"

"Cops," says La Tessica, "dumb cops."

"Your tone stinks, Angie," says Julius. "Angie gets into serious trouble, Tess, who does she come cryin' to?"

"Dumb cops," says La Tessica, "two moron cops, who unlike her brush their teeth on a regular basis."

"I brush my teeth on a regular basis."

"Oh, yeah? Think we don't know the truth? Don't trash dumb cops of constrained cognitive capacity. Know such words, Angie? Cognitive? Didn't think so. Let's go to lunch, Juju."

Angie says, as they leave, "Gina, Jackie is being seriously discussed for the Big Needle. Take him now because tomorrow might be too late. And please put in a good word for me with the Titan of the Industry, Big Frank himself."

"No worries, Ang," says Gina, leash in hand, as she, the dog, and the two big men—taking her offer for a ride to Manhattan— make their way through the terminal to her limo-in-waiting, where Blackie a.k.a. Jackie climbs onto her lap.

2

They struggle through the revolving door, then up two steps, bouncing their luggage onto the floor of the lobby. At the reception desk, Jade Miranda welcomes Eliot Conte and Antonio Robinson to the twenty-two storeys, at Vanderbilt Avenue, of The Yale Club of New York City.

"I have a reservation," says Conte, "made by Doctor Harry Gallatin, on behalf of Eliot Conte. That would be me. Now and then."

Robinson says, "He thinks he's funny."

Conte's self-lacerating humor had captured the heart of his heart surgeon, who saw in Conte a brother in Hell, and so had arranged five nights at the Club for Conte and spouse. That's to say, he told the reservation clerk, for Conte and his most intimate assassin.

Unimpressed by Conte's wit, Jade touches her computer and says, "Five nights for Mr. and Mrs. Conte." She glances sidelong at Robinson.

"My wife," Conte says, throwing his arm around Robinson's shoulders, "kept his maiden name."

"The wife," says Robinson, "the formidable Catherine Cruz. Which to this point I am not."

Jade, with another furtive glance at Robinson: "All expenses, including meals and drinks, to be charged to the account of Doctor Gallatin."

"The formidable Catherine Cruz," Conte says, "couldn't make it. My friend wishes to assume wifely obligations in all departments." (Massaging Robinson's shoulders.)

Jade smiles brilliantly.

"The humor returns," Robinson says, "but you should've seen him on the flight down. A leaf in a hurricane."

Quickly pivoting from professional welcome to professional concern, Jade says, "Gentlemen, I'm obligated to enforce a new protocol at the Club, instituted one week ago. I must ask if either of you have in the past 30 days returned from a foreign country."

"Yes," Conte says, "both of us. We flew in from Syracuse this morning. Which of course is not the foreign country we drove from to reach Syracuse."

Jade says, "Canada, I presume?"

Robinson says, "Utica, sweetheart. Utica, New York."

Jade says, "I appreciate a pair of comedians in these times. I take it that the answer to my question is no."

"So the Yale Club," Robinson says, "The Yale Club of New York City—"

"Yes," says Jade.

"It becomes suddenly like a hospital? Because a couple of old ladies got this thing in Seattle and croaked at the age of 117? From this thing, this flu?"

"Our advisors," Jade says, "at the Yale Medical School, recommend vigilance. They believe that—"

Conte breaks in: "This Chinese thing. It's going to hit the fan? Everywhere, according to Yale?"

Jade says, "We're committed to maximum vigilance on behalf of our guests."

"So," Conte says, "if we came in from China in the last 30 days? And we told you the truth? Then what?"

"We would need, with regret, to deny you our hospitality, but let's not imagine the nightmare. You're here from Utica, not China. Once more, welcome to The Yale Club of New York City, commonly known as The Yale Club."

Jade, looking at computer, "Gentlemen, I'm afraid we have a problem. When Doctor Gallatin contacted us he requested a single room, with a queen-sized bed, on the assumption that—" she looks up—"you do see where I'm going with this."

"Just so you know," Robinson says, "neither of us is light in the loafers."

"Sorry?"

"Old saying from the homophobic era: Light in the loafers. Want to watch me walk?"

Jade nearly succeeds in keeping a straight face.

"My wife," Conte says, "couldn't leave her colleagues in the lurch. It's tech week for *Cat on a Hot Tin Roof*. She's Maggie the Cat and my friend here is the substitute in the queen-sized bed."

Robinson leaning over the counter, closer to Jade: "How about two rooms? Or at least a king-sized bed? Less of an intimate situation. As you see, we're big. We're very big."

Conte says, "What you cannot observe with the naked eye, you can imagine."

Stifling an outright laugh, Jade says, "Doctor Gallatin authorized only one room. I have a king for you two kings, but it won't be ready until after lunch, when I can guarantee by 3 pm, official check-in time. So sorry, gentlemen, for the inconvenience."

Robinson: "Four and a half hours to kill?"

"In an hour and a half you'll have your choice of lunch in the Tap Room on the third floor, where your jeans are not acceptable, unless Arturo is feeling excessively liberal, or the Grill Room on the mezzanine, a few steps below the Tap Room, where your tight jeans are welcomed, especially by Alonso and Abdul. The Lounge on the second floor is open, but the bar is not until noon, although Akash is in there now cleaning up and setting up. Since he and I go way back—"

"You go way back with Akash?" Conte says.

Robinson says, "She's too young to go way back. With anyone."

"See those stairs?" says Jade. "Take them to the second floor. I'll make a call to Akash, who'll be waiting to make you big dudes drinks of your choice. In addition, there's the library on the fourth floor, where you may enjoy quiet time for reading, writing, or closing your eyes and dozing off."

"I love the odor in the morning," Conte says, "of decaying old books."

"Bank on it, boys. Akash will serve you soon."

They check their luggage. Consider taking the elevator to the lounge on the second floor, but decide not to give in to life in the final phase and instead mount the stairs, with distress almost perfectly concealed.

Robinson enters the enormous room while Conte heads to the Men's Room to appease his compromised prostate. Robinson orders a Negroni for himself and a diet coke with a slice of lime for Conte.

Conte returns to the enormous room, where a fall from its ceiling would guarantee instant death—where the windows, could they be opened wide, would permit comfortable access to a helicopter, and whose walls are dominated by gigantic paintings of historic Yalies, one of whom Robinson calls Clitin, the other two pronounced by Conte as Butches 1 and 2.

Conte says, "Suddenly off beer? What is that?"

Robinson raises his glass in a toast: "Thought I'd give it a shot. A drink invented by your people in honor of my people. A Negroni. In honor of us who used to be called Negroes. We ought to go back to that. Negroes for Negroni. Vice-versa."

Conte toasts him. They touch glasses. Conte sips, making a face, says, "This is off. Way off." Goes to bar and returns with another drink.

Robinson says, "That doesn't look like—what is that?" He leans over. Conte offers him a sniff.

Conte sips his new drink.

Robinson says, "What? Seven plus years down the toilet?"

Conte sips.

"The flight destroy your nerves? That it?"

Conte stares at his glass.

"Johnnie Walker?"

Conte stares at his glass.

"Black," Conte says.

"What?"

"Get it right, Robby. Johnnie Walker Black."

"Talk to me, El."

Conte drains his glass.

"You were a recovering drunk for over seven years."

Conte looks into empty glass.

"Now you're just a drunk."

Conte says nothing.

"Wanna destroy yourself and family? Talk to me."

Conte goes to the bar. Returns with another Johnnie Walker Black. Guzzling Scotch. Conte is heading to a bottom below the bottom.

Robinson says, "At the reception desk you were your old self. Now all of a sudden this? Gonna confide in me?"

"Akash has a bottle of Johnnie Walker Blue. Highest quality of all Johnnies. Seventy-five bucks for two fingers, but I couldn't take advantage of the good Doctor Gallatin's largesse. Akash offers two fingers on the house. I accept. Blue. I don't sip. I drain it. Unimaginable. This Black will do."

"Blue, black, who gives a—? You prefer to hide rather than to confide?"

"If the gloves don't fit, you must acquit. Shall we cut the black jive?"

"Catherine?"

"Yes."

"You and Catherine?"

"Yes."

"What's the issue?"

"A third party."

"Someone I know? I'll break his legs."

"No."

"Some guy I *don't* know?"

"No."

"Where does he live? You telling me a woman? Catherine's hetero. She's hot. She's hetero. She's one of the last heteros among the eleven genders."

"Not a woman."

"A trans? Whichever way? The latest type of sex bomb? They say a nuclear weapon. I can appreciate. Not saying I—"

"No."

Conte doesn't sip. He knocks it back. Two blacks and a blue on an empty stomach at 11 a.m. Stone-cold sober. Stone-cold killer. As in his old alcoholic days, his drinking to deep drunkenness takes him to a level of sobriety beyond sobriety. A place of icy will and clarity of purpose. A prelude to an eruption of violence that no one could ever see coming—not even himself. Like that time—like so many other times—when he hoisted a man on a train—hoisted high a man abusing his wife and baby to bruises—across the aisle from quiet and expressionless Conte, who arose slowly, without a word, and hoisted him by the neck, shaking him like a rag doll. The man fouling himself in fear, that day on the train when Conte was at peak strength, alcohol-fueled. *That* Conte, the one on the train, now physically gone after years of heart disease, now 74 and only six weeks past open-heart surgery. Gone except in spirit and desire.

Robinson says, "How long you keeping me in the dark?"

"She's having an affair with the fantasy she's nourished since she was a teenager. A life in the theater. As an actress."

He goes to the bar and returns with his third Johnnie Black. (Let's not forget the blue.) He's acquired the perfect peace that booze always gave. He sips. He's happy. He knows who he is. He sips. The peace beyond understanding.

"What's the harm in that?" Robinson wants to know. "Her performance with Utica Players in *Streetcar*—she was a terrific Stella, though a little old for the role. Totally sexy, obviously."

"The director's brother was visiting his sister, who was directing his favorite play. To support her fantasy of directorial fame. Another Utica girl not ever headed to New York theatrical stardom. He told Catherine at the cast party after opening night how impressive she was, she told me this, and that she should see him in New York because he thought she had special talent, a career if she wanted one. He told her he'd guarantee her work. On Broadway. That was last Spring. When she finishes with *Cat on a Hot Tin Roof* she intends to see this man who is about our age. When we return to Utica, Robby, I take care of our daughter and she comes down here to see him and her suddenly realized fantasy."

"This guy's a big producer?"

"Yes."

"His payment for making her fantasy real?"

"I'll talk to him this afternoon."

"Talk?"

"I feel good."

"You're too old for this. We're too old."

"I feel very good."

"It's almost noon. Shall we go to the Grill Room?"

"You go."

"You don't want lunch?"

"I'll go."

"When?"

"After."

3

Detective Vince Ventura of the Midtown Manhattan 17th Precinct decided that the limo-driver, who'd made the trip in question from La Guardia, would be the last he'd interview—in the room where the detective had personally installed harsh, high wattage bulbs. Because Ventura assumed that Angel Rodriguez was a dispassionate observer—potentially a corrective to the testimony of his three passengers—and no doubt a Catholic (like himself) and a fan (as he was) of the New York Yankees, with a name similar to a Yankee star of renown. Ventura would say, "Call me, Vince." He'd say, "Do your friends, Angel, call you A-Rod?" He would interview Gina Rendonello only if the testimony of the others would enable him to tighten the noose around her sexy throat—and cause her to cough up the object of his long-held desire.

Detective Vince Ventura intended to relax Rodriguez to the point where Angel would feel he was in kind hands. Vince would take him on a short stroll, that's what he'd do, like a good dog on a leash, from the station at 167 East 51st, for a drink at the Waldorf Astoria, whose entrance and bar area reminded him very strongly of the interior of St. Peter's. Yes, Angel, *that* St. Peter's. Have you been there? No? I'll send you a color postcard. Vince would tell him that he'd been to St. Peter's on three occasions, the latest this year to celebrate his 35th wedding anniversary with the surprising Marie Rose Ventura, née Convertino.

Detective Ventura regards himself as a devout nonpracticing Catholic, who prays weekly to St. Jude, Patron Saint of Hopeless Causes, "that I, Vince, who you know extremely well what I have

to have because I am hopeless, I don't pray, I totally *beseech* thee—
it's about time, right? you should get me the suck… the sweet
sucker of Heaven. Forget about my numerous sufferings except
for the one I've been asking you for, for relief for, for sixteen endless years for, for which you have not relieved me of for whatever
reason known to your Holy Self and possibly the Blessed Virgin
Mary, who has her Son by the ear, which she constantly twists at
will, that I may bless God with the Elect throughout eternity. St.
Jude! Cut me some slack! Amen."

On their 35th at St. Peter's, Marie Rose Ventura had decided
to go to confession, which she complains "they no longer call
'confession,' they call it the 'Sacrament of Reconciliation,'" words
that Marie Rose found, as she often said, "repulsive," because she
had no desire to be reconciled—"to nothing, Vince, and nobody,
Vince, except to you, at frequent times." She wanted to confess.
Period. If she died immediately after "confession" she'd go straight
up to the Lord because her soul would be clean. Reconciliation?
"Liberal Catholic crap."

When she emerged from the dark box at St. Peter's, she said
to Vince, "This priest? With him you can handle your shame. He
doesn't understand English. He kept saying, louder and louder,
Cosa? Che hai fatto? (What did you do?) Whatever sins you want
to conceal, don't bother, including the worst ones, including murder which you never did. Right? When I finished in there he goes,
Cento Padre Nostro." (100 Our Fathers.) So Vince stepped into the
dark box for the first time since he couldn't remember when and
confessed his worst sin—that he really wanted a particular person
dead. He thought about it constantly. Dead. And the priest, Father
Destino, said, "*Figlio mio! Non me ne frega un cazzo!*" Which Vince
and Marie Rose knew as a brutal vulgarity: Father Destino was
saying, About your sins, my son, I don't give a fuck!

Detective Vince had been informed by his supervisor that
limo-driver Angel Rodriguez had taken three passengers from La
Guardia to Manhattan. Two men to The Yale Club and a female
to an apartment on the upper East Side, at The Royal York, a few

blocks north of the precinct station. Ventura contacted law enforcement in Utica and learned that the men were more than old pals—they were brothers in all but blood. He had little interest in either, despite their provocative Utica histories. He would talk to them, but only as a means to the end of unbuttoning this female who was of thrilling interest. This hot Gina Rendonello, the favorite niece of Big Frank's notorious younger brother James— Red Rendonello, as he was known for his red hair—a nickname which he detested (though he liked "Red Alert") who had fled the Bronx sixteen years ago, on the night before his secretly guarded indictment was about to drop on eleven counts of racketeering and nineteen counts of murder. Twelve murders delegated to his second in command, an Italian-American called by Red, The Patriot. The remaining seven slayings he had assigned to himself because he was nothing like those pussy Mafia Dons, who delegated death to their enforcers. No, Red Alert was a hands-on kind of guy. He did the seven executions with his actual hands, ungloved, fingernails radically pared so that afterwards he'd not have to get under them with a butter knife.

The man with the flaming ginger top was the elusive Red Whale of Ventura's obsession, who'd not been seen since his disappearance sixteen years ago, who had grown up, like Ventura, in the Belmont section of the Bronx, the true Little Italy of New York, long before and after Mulberry Street went down the tourist toilet. Arthur Avenue in the Bronx remains. Unstained.

At the 17th and around the five boroughs Vince Ventura was known with a sad shake of the head. How he happened to be assigned the case involving Angel Rodriguez had everything to do with his reputation as Johnny One Note. The case, as such, had little, if any, discernible merit or urgency and would not have been taken seriously except for the willingness of the Chief of Detectives to indulge Ventura's singular focus on his former Bronx neighbor.

Unlike his colleagues at the 17th, the Chief was moved by Ventura's obsession. He thought Vince extreme, perhaps a bit cracked, but also the most selfless devotee of justice he had known in his 37 years on the force.

Vince understood that he was seen as a painful case, at best, and, at worst, with a little contempt. Not a week would pass, it was said, when he could not be heard regaling bored colleagues with his theory of Red Rendonello's plastic surgery, the shaved head, the full beard, the new identity documents. He knew, he said, from way back in our Bronx days, that Red was a beach-fanatic, who would walk his dog for miles in all seasons alongside the dying wavelets on crescent-shaped Orchard Beach, the Bronx Riviera. It was against the rules to bring a dog to Orchard Beach, but who would risk a re-arranged face for telling him so? Vince was certain that Red would be found on the warm coast of Southern California, in the Los Angeles area, probably Santa Monica, because Red loved the L.A. Lakers. On the cliffs of Santa Monica, Red could look North to Pacific Palisades, as he took in another crescent-shaped coast line.

The case in question had come to the 17th via a complaint lodged by a celebrity Broadway producer, who claimed to have been accosted by a cadaverous-looking man named Eliot Conte and told by this Conte to leave his wife alone, never again to be in contact with her in any way, if the celebrity, in Conte's words, wanted to attend his next birthday on this broken earth. The Chief of Detectives had Conte brought in, who told him he was in New York with his friend Antonio Robinson. Conte offered that they had been driven to The Yale Club in a limo with one Gina Rendonello, who was, he said, believe it or not, the daughter of the head of Delta Airlines, Big Frank Rendonello.

The Chief did not bother to question Conte further about the alleged threat to the Broadway Big Shot. He'd heard all he needed to hear, dismissed Conte, and texted Ventura. Because at last Vince would have a flimsy, though legitimate reason for grilling so-called innocent Gina.

Sixteen years ago, the rumor in law enforcement had spread to the media: that no one knew the pending indictment was about to drop on Red except the Police Commissioner. A reasonable theory of conspiracy, among the men in blue, said that Big Frank had been tipped off by the commissioner himself—a theory that gained credibility a few years later when the commish was fired and charged with bilking the department's budget in order (among other things) to remodel his kitchen and three bathrooms and purchase round trip first-class airfare to Dublin for himself, wife, four adult children, and seven grandchildren. Incarceration was a certainty. The Police Commissioner escaped prison with a self-administered bullet to the brain.

Ventura embraced the theory and elaborated it into a detailed fiction, of whose truth he was convinced: Big Frank had no doubt alerted brother Jimmy, who knew he was under surveillance (when wasn't he?) and Red planned his flight from the law on the night he was told by Big Frank that his violent career would end without bail, life in a super-max prison in Colorado, where a number of inmates (with the assistance of a bribed guard) would be eager to make themselves legends in the annals of crime by killing him. Jimmy made one phone call and his plan was secured.

That night, Jimmy R walked Tiger, his mini-Schnauzer, at sundown, because he always did. Red felt deep love for the dogs of his difficult life. When it came time to put them down, he took them to the vet for the Final Needle, and he wept. From the vet to Hartsdale Pet Cemetery weeping he drove, to purchase a hillside plot and monument for the marvelous Fortney, who preceded Tiger.

None knew with the exception of Gina Rendonello that after Fortney's death, Red saw a psychiatrist three times per week for a year. (Xanax. Klonopin.) Uncle Jimmy's job would easily accommodate his shrink appointments. His major duties, she understood, were performed at night. Gina was the child he never had, whom he loved possibly even more than he had loved Fortney, may he rest in peace. Gina R, at 17, even then towered over her uncle who stood 5'8" in shoes. Uncle Red (she alone could get away with calling him Red) once told her that he had purchased perpetual care for all his dogs "in case something happens to me, God forbid, I want their graves maintained with flowers at whatever cost to me forever."

This is how Ventura sees it, has seen it for sixteen years, and will always see it. Red with devious intention walking Tiger from his unassuming house next to the playground on Belmont Ave, walking east, to East 187th Street. Slow, halting walk, Tiger lifting his leg many times. On 187th visiting first DeLillo's Pastry Shop and then Egidio's. (Fact according to store clerks at aforementioned venerable establishments.)

Ventura seeing it vividly in full color: Red's entrance into the two pastry havens producing massive fear. The owner of DeLillo's knowing, as everyone on the Avenue knew, that Red abominated sweets. Consequently, had never been seen crossing the threshold of any pastry shop in the area.

The owner of DeLillo's saying, "Yo! Jim! What a tremendous surprise!"

Jim replying, "Yeah."

"What can I get for you? On the house, Jim! On the house."

Jim pointing to the sfogliatelle, flashing two fingers.

The owner saying, "Two?"

"Yeah."

The owner giving him three.

Same scene playing out at Egidio's. Two cannoli requested, three given. "On the house! Because your money's no good here, Jim. No offense, Jim."

Jimmy departing, holding two small white bags in one hand and the leash in the other: Heading east on 187th, slowly, haltingly—much Tiger-leg-lifting. Twice, Tiger peeing in a squat, thereby causing Red Alert to meditate with piercing anxiety on the unspeakable thought that his fierce Tiger was displaying gender fluidity by pissing like a bitch.

Always east on 187th, but unsurveilled since leaving Egidio's because in their ignorance of Red's dietary requirements the two student volunteers from the Police Academy concluded that Red

tonight is only about walking "his constant pissing dog and eating dessert." No point in wasting time following this maniac.
And so they leave the job as Jim, out of sight now, dumps the
bags of pastries into a sewer somewhere east of Arthur Avenue.
The volunteers file their report, which years later will be retrieved
from the department's archive by assiduous Vince: Walked dog,
bought pastries on the way. Another boring stake out without
consequences.

Red Rendonello, a unique presence on Arthur Avenue—frequently seen cruising the Belmont streets, but looking like no one
you'd see there on any given day among the full-bodied—do not
call them fat, do not say rotund—these olive-complected, vigorous men and women who speak Italian as often as English and
kiss each other on the cheek. There he'd be, pale-faced, blue-eyed,
his blazing straight hair slicked back with not a strand out of
place—145 pounds of flexible steel, no trace of belly, washboard
abdominals, ramrod posture—on the run back from Orchard
Beach where he does six miles per day, six days per week before
returning to his weight-lifting regime. Or in late afternoon there
he'd be, striding to the stores he most frequented, Casa della
Mozzarella, Madonia Bakery, the Calabria Pork Store—the latter
a salumeria that might have been designed by Federico Fellini—
whose vast ceiling, every inch of it, formed an unbroken spectacle,
a chandelier of several hundred hanging prosciutto, salami, sop-
pressata, pepperoni, cotechino, culatello, various salsicce and other
hanging delights of no name—no one knew the names—not the
clerks, not the store owner dozing in the back room, mouth open
in his recliner and snoring at a decibel level to scare the Devil—
not even the owner's wife, who knew everything.

From his rackets Red had reaped many millions, the great
sum a source of impregnable financial security, but his deepest
source of happiness his money could not buy: it was what the
Madonia Bakery, the Casa Della Mozzarella, and the Calabria
Pork Store together triggered in his mind—a vision of overflow-
ing and never-ending abundance, to nourish the flesh, yes, but

nourish what cannot be subject to the ills and the deterioration of the body: nourishment of the spirit against and beyond time and death itself.

As Vince envisions him heading east on 187th, unsurveilled, this is what in his mind he will always see: Red reaching the corner of 187th and Southern Blvd. Across the boulevard, the Bronx Zoo. To be met at the corner by Gina in the starless dark of an overcast night. (Yes, overcast: Vince knew, he'd gone back into weather archives for New York City.) And Gina there parked illegally on Southern Blvd (Vince in imaginative full flight) in her honey gold vintage '65 Mustang. (Fact: she had one: how did Vince know? Deep he'd gone into DMV records.) From there driving Red Alert not to one of the major New York area airports, but to the least likely to be watched: Westchester County Airport and Tradewind Aviation, where he would board a flight to Martha's Vineyard. (Vince's supreme fiction, but he would bet the rare antique sewing machine that his wife had inherited from her great grandmother, which Marie Rose Ventura née Convertino loved more than she loved Vince, whom she loved a great deal.) Then from the Vineyard to Boston's Logan, 5½ hours via ferry and a bus. Then a flight to the Far West. It's obvious.

Though it matched, Detective Ventura could not prove that the '65 Mustang captured on video at Westchester County was Gina's—because the video had not captured an image of the license plate. Gina was the key. Gina knew what her father, Big Frank, did not. She knew where Red was living. Obviously, she would not tell Big Frank. She no doubt was in periodic phone contact over the years. Doubtless, she had visited Red on the West Coast as she routinely signed on for onerous cross-country flights with three stops. She always knew. You, Gina.

What choice did Red have? He left Tiger in the Mustang at Westchester County. On one of Gina's visits to Southern California she would have broken the news of Tiger's fate and Red would have said, "He passed?" And Gina would have embraced him and said, "Yes, Uncle Jimmy." And Red would have broken down. And Gina would have attempted to console, but Gina would have failed to relieve her uncle of his agony. Who would have said to her, I am consumed by the thought of death. What is it? I have given death many times, but what is it? Who would in his grief tell her of the time when Tiger, a year old, got into a cabinet beneath the kitchen sink and ate a Brillo pad and drank cleaning fluid. Of how two vets (Red needed a second opinion) pronounced Tiger irreversibly death-bound, though of course, Mr. Rendonello, you could try the Cornell Veterinary School, and Red had driven Tiger nonstop at unsafe speed to Cornell where after five weeks of treatment and $33,435 Tiger was saved. "Gina," he would say, "thank God I left you enough cold cash to have the dignified thing at Hartsdale in perpetuity." Red, like Vince, was a devout nonpracticing Catholic, with conservative views on abortion and assisted suicide, who prayed to St. Jude for "favors which I need quick," favors that St. Jude could not grant because, if they were, St. Jude himself would be cast down into the Everlasting Fire.

Detective Ventura thought about it and thought about it. He consulted not the Chief of Detectives, but Marie Rose Ventura and together they concluded it would be foolish at this point to interrogate the fair Gina. He didn't yet know enough, Marie Rose said, "to put her tits in a vise." He'd only spook her, she'd surmise his intention, her guard would go up, never to be let down and he would never locate Red and put him away. He needed to talk seriously to those two guys from Utica and then to Angel Rodriguez. Extract what he could, seize and file away any odd detail in their stories—something they said but didn't intend to say "and eventually, Vince, you open Gina wide and work her over on the table in the interrogation room."

He was not, whatever his colleagues thought, dumb or psychologically unsound. He was just Vince Ventura.

4

He called her his Secretary of State—she who had insisted that she be permitted to watch and listen though the miked, one-way window as her husband conducted the interview with Antonio Robinson. Without hesitation, the Chief of Detectives agreed to assuage the Secretary's need. Because unlike his scornful charges, Chief Michael Molloy not only has a soft spot for Vince, but also an unrequited hard spot for Marie Rose, ever since she had turned him down for their high school Prom. Though comfortably married (so forth) and the Irish Catholic father of seven children and grandfather of fourteen, the Chief continues to nourish, at age 58, a forty-one-year fantasy "till death do us part," as he once mumbled at the kitchen sink in a romantically abstracted state, in the vicinity of his clueless wife—who mistook the referent and hugged him tenderly from behind, as he washed the dinner dishes.

When asked by the young priest, in the dark of the confessional, if he'd entertained and "savored impure thoughts," Michael Molloy said, "Father, many times." And the priest replied, "Who am I to judge? This is, after all, the twenty-first century. The Lord of Mercy gifted us, in his off hours, with imagination, so much the better to enjoy what we need not practice. Let us say, sex beyond, far beyond, the boundaries. Let us say, for certain, murder of our numerous enemies and their total obliteration from the surface of the earth. Be not afraid. Embrace what in His wisdom the Good Lord has granted."

As he left the confessional, liberated—as he walked home on the neon streets of Queens, Michael Malloy luxuriated in his erotic flights, as in a warm bath, even the very next day strolling hand in hand with his wife in Central Park, where he had decades before proposed to Betty Jean on bended knee, the Irish Catholic mother of his seven children—or nine, as she would say, and said many times, who had lost two to miscarriage.

No one at the 17th Precinct would ever care to observe "Vinny the Obsessed" at work, as he sought impossible links to Red Rendonello from beaten prostitutes, petty thieves, and abusive husbands. The Chief himself had a meeting that morning at City Hall and would be denied the opportunity of standing close behind Marie Rose at the window. Marie Rose would stand alone—watching and listening and intervening in the event that Vince seemed on the verge of losing control of his purpose, who had insisted, the maniac, at 5:45 that morning, on having the second of their twice weekly events. Usually, a little of *this*, a little of *that*. At 5:45 a.m.: the whole enchilada.

At breakfast she tells him, "We shouldn't have done it, Vincent. Look at you! Like you're on Valium or one of those other narcotics. You hear a knock on the one-way window? It's me saying come out for emergency consultation."

"Twice a week, for 35 years, you say I'm a fresh piece and I say you're the all time sex machine. But *today*?! When possibly closing in on Red? Your face is swollen up with blood. You look like a lion full of raw meat who's about to hit the sack for a week."

At a red light on the way to the 17th, as Vince—a mediocre driver, at best—sits in the front passenger seat, she turns to him and says, "Two cups of coffee black before you start on this African-American, this Robinson. Stifle your tendency to refer to 'you people.' You're hunting this Red Animal for what? Sixteen years? I pray to the Virgin that you didn't this morning at the break of dawn ejaculate Red Rendonello out of your mind."

At 7:50 they arrive at the 17th to execute the plan devised the night before by the Secretary of State and approved reflexively by her husband. Reflexively? In other words, thoughtlessly—as he had approved through the decades all of his wife's suggestions, trivial and major. In self-delusion, he thinks of himself as a husband of independent will, when in truth, for 35 years, he has surrendered, in tranquility, all will in all areas with the exception of the bedroom, where his powers put him, as she once said in the afterglow of her satiation, "in a league of your own."

Vince feared to ask, from the profound well of his Italian jealousy, about the players in other leagues. He never asked her the overwhelming question and she never asked him where and when he had honed his woman-shattering craft. She never knew because he never revealed that she was his first and, God-willing, his last. What he gave was wholly the expression of his desire for her body and soul: a division whose reality he would not comprehend, much less acknowledge.

Marie Rose tells Vince that the harsh lights in the room of interrogation must be changed. And they were. By Vince on a wobbly ladder, her steadying hands cradling his ass. And the new lights are soft. Fresh flowers, she says, must be ordered and promptly delivered. And they were: an array of roses of different colors. Two dozen pastries, she says, from Egidio's on Arthur Avenue. That's way up in the Bronx, Marie! Marie replies, When is Jackie Robinson supposed to get here? 9:30, right? So we have time. Send one of your cruisers up there, Vincent. Make a list, Vincent: sfogliatelle, tiramisu, panettone, cannoli, biscotti (the anisette-flavored type), assorted cookies. Two dozen. Marie! Two *dozen*? Use that head of yours, she says. Bring in the coffee pot and start brewing at 9:20. The aromas. The visuals. The gentle lighting. See my point, Vince? The devastating impact on the wary Mr. Robinson? Take off the tie. Good. Let me muss up your fabulous hair like this. Good. The sleek look is professional. Which we don't want. We want the neighborhood guy. Go wash your face good with soap. Because we don't want the cologne ambiance. See what I'm saying? Stop with the hands, Vince. What is this I feel here in my hand? A beautiful salami in your pocket? No. Not the table. Not now. No. Interview this Robinson. Don't even *think* interrogation. He was a law enforcement man? Think conversation among intimate birds.

* * *

9:27: Antonio Robinson is ushered into Ventura's lair. Vince, stealthy animal, had prepared. Had combed the Utica and university background. The years on the force before Robinson rose to Chief. The years as Chief. The black Chief so well-liked, so admired, in a town of classic ethnics, whose discomfort with African-Americans was historically given. The Italians and the Poles of Utica loved him, whose life was scandal-free. And who did not know of him in his athletic years of national football fame? The stories of his prowess and thrilling breakaway dashes to daylight. The photos. The comparisons to the greatest running backs in the history of college football. The photos of young Robinson in his prime, of a body that can only be called beautiful, thought Ventura, whose insatiable heterosexual requirements never caused him to repress his admiration for the exceptional bodies of outstanding athletes, of each and every gender. Then the career-destroying injury.

Though he should not have been, Vince was shocked by the Robinson who came through the door. It wasn't the obesity and limping gait. It was the face. Whose face was this face that bore no trace of Antonio Robinson, All-American? Those photos that Vince looks at too often of his parents in their courting time. Those of Marie Rose when he met her, and of himself, at 25, against the face he sees each morning in the (mourning) mirror. All images of the beginning of the plot, the movement toward unbeauty and death—are they the cause, Detective Ventura, of your undiminished sexual vitality as you close in on 60? Your old man panic? The hard cock against the approaching end?

—Chief Robinson! Welcome to the 17th!

—Yeah.

—Your cooperation in this sensitive matter—

—What sensitive?

—We'll get to that.

—What is this? (*Gesturing toward table of flowers and pastries.*)

The Ladies' F-ing Book Club?

—Funny. (*With forced laugh.*)

(Marie Rose: Hands to face.)

—All my years no detective of mine ever offered anything except a cup of lousy coffee. What is this?

—Starbuck's Deluxe Delight. This'll be quick, Chief. Make yourself comfortable.

(Ventura sits. Robinson hesitates. Sits.

Marie Rose wants to knock, but restrains herself.

Robinson sizing up Vince's physique is reminded of his glory days. How does this guy at his age keep his body? Robinson can't imagine the 25 daily pushups, the forty daily situps, the 50 jumping jacks, daily, the 35 years of twice weekly sexercise. 3500 erotic events.)

—All of this, Detective Ventura—the flowers, the sweets, the coffee, the soft lights. Gonna propose to me? You want something? My cherry? You're not sure I'll give it up. Am I right?

(Marie Rose knocks. Vince excuses himself. Instructs him to change the subject: Get to the limo from La Guardia. Vince claims he was about to. She says, Don't make me knock again, Vincent.)

Robinson says, as Vince re-enters, Talk to your supervisor, Detective? Vince says, In a way. Vince pushes the box of goodies from Egidio's toward Robinson, who pushes it back saying, Not in the mood. Vince says, Me neither, as he takes a cannoli and goes to town on it. Vince says, We received a serious complaint yesterday from a big Broadway producer about your friend Eliot Conte. This producer is a known pig for years. If you lived in this town, Chief, you read about him in the *Post* all the time, page 6, the alleged behavior against women. If your friend scared him? The threat involved a promise of lethal violence—a crime, I don't need to tell you—but I'm not interested. I chalk it up to the understandable outburst of a husband toward a creep of the entertainment world. Who cares? One person's word against another. A legal sinkhole. Robinson says, Eliot Conte's my friend since childhood. I assure you he's not, never has been, never *will* be capable of physical violence. Vince says, This here, the two of us, is not about your friend. Robinson says, Yeah. Let's cut to the chase. I can walk out the door right now. I'm here only out of courtesy. Cop to cop. Vince says, You walk, you walk, but I'd appreciate a few more minutes.

Robinson says, Aren't you going to exercise the protocol? Vince says, What protocol? Robinson says, The one in place at The Yale Club of New York City. Vince says, There's another Yale Club somewhere else? Where is it? What protocol? Robinson says, as Vince starts on cannoli #2, You won't keep your terrific figure eating those things. Vince says, These things? (Holding up the cannoli.) They're more health conscious than the elitist morons of America can understand. Robinson says, You include me in that demographic? Vince says, It's not a partisan polarization.

Robinson says, Have I been out of the country in the last 30 days on some international junket? Vince says, How would I know? Have you? Hope to God not Italy or Iran in these times. (*Marie Rose is happy. Her husband is sneaky. Who knew?*) Robinson says, The Yale Club of New York City is overreacting about admitting into their midst people who have come down with this new thing. Which is why the hysterical protocol. Vince says, What thing? Robinson says, What those two old broads in Seattle got in a Nursing Home and died miserable deaths from. Vince says (*taking in the final chunk of cannoli*), That thing. Right. Robinson says, Your lungs drown you on dry land. Vince says, This Chinese disease? Which those Chinese artificially invented through science? And sent it here to ream it up this country? (*Marie Rose feels immediate pride in Vince's clever moves. He's moving in for the kill.*) Robinson says, Seattle, the home of those elitist m-f-ers, those constant coffee swillers. The count this morning in Seattle is up to 17. Old f-ers, like me and my friend Eliot Conte. Sooner or later we go, one way or the other. Vince says, Were you in Seattle? Or some foreign country? In the last 30 days? Yes or no? Robinson says, No to Seattle. Yes to a foreign country because you New Yorkers with your superiority complex consider Upstate

New York a foreign country. Think we upstaters don't know how you downstaters think? So what's the underlying topic on your mind, Detective Ventura, beside two cannoli and now a hefty almond cookie? Vince says, I did my research. Neither you or your friend went to Yale. How'd you get in? Robinson says, Dr. Harry Gallatin. Another story. Maybe some other time. What do you want from me?

Vince says, Tell me about the ride into Manhattan. The conversation. Everything to the best of your recollection. The memorable, the trivial. Especially the trivial. Robinson says, Nothing memorable. All trivial. Vince says, Beautiful. In the limo, the seating arrangements. Start with the driver. Robinson says, The driver drove from the driver's seat—starting at La Guardia all the way to The Yale Club of New York City the driver drove without changing his seat, as a licensed limo driver. Vince says, You got me, Chief. I said something ridiculous. Leaving out of it the driver's function inside the limo, the driver's name was? Robinson says, Something Rodriguez. Yeah, Andy Rodriguez. Or maybe *Angus* Rodriguez. Vince says, Might it be *Angel* rather than Andy or Angus? Robinson says, Yeah. Angel. Which those people pronounce An-*Hell*, if I'm not mistaken. Vince says, You're not mistaken. When you arrived at The Yale Club, the one in New York City, did Angel Rodriguez exit and get replaced, by any chance, with another driver? Robinson says, To the best of my recollection, Angus was not replaced. He dropped me and Eliot and went on with the girl. Gina Rendonello. I don't know where he would have dropped her off. It never came up inside the limo. Where she lives. Vince says, Upper East Side. The Royal York. A fact. Good. Thank you.

Vince says, Let's back this account up a little. The total seating arrangement. Robinson says, Next to the driver—Vince cuts him off, In the front passenger seat? Robinson says, Detective. Vince says, Yes? Robinson says, Detective. Vince says, Lay it on me without mercy. Robinson says, Who's on first? Vince says, Pardon me? Robinson says, Sorry. Old comedy routine. Abbot and Costello.

Vince says, Who? Robinson says, Correct. Who. YouTube. Check
it out. Vince says, The back seat arrangement in the limo. Who is
where, exactly? Robinson says, Bud Abbot and Lou Costello will
assist you. YouTube. I sat behind Conte, who sat in the front passenger seat next to the driver. She and he sat behind the driver.
Vince says, She and *he*? There was a *fourth* male in the limo? Who
sat in the back seat? I was informed by unimpeachable sources
that there were a total of *four* in the limo, including the driver.
You're telling me now that there was a *fifth*? A total of *five*, including the driver?

Robinson says, Let's walk through this step by step and I'll
specify who is in the limo. The driver. Conte. Yours truly. Gina
Rendonello. And another big black male, who is called Blackie or
Jackie. Vince says, For the record, what does the big black male,
who is not you, call himself? For the record. Including *surname*.
For the record, Chief. Robinson says, He doesn't, who is sitting
in Gina's lap, to the best of my knowledge, call himself anything.
The odds are very good that he has no surname and does not long
for one. Vince says, Far out! Robinson says, He's a big black male
dog. (*Marie Rose knocking hard, 3 times. Vince looking up, shaking his
head. Knocks again, 3 times. Harder. Vince looks up with a smile. She's
the Secretary of State, but he at long last is the Commander-in-Chief.*)

Robinson says, I once sat where you sit for years. Your Chief
of Detectives is very concerned on the other side of the one-way,
but you feel all is going well. A big black male dog in her lap.
Un-neutered, I have to tell you. Excited in her lap. Vince says, He
still had a pair? Hopefully still does? Robinson says, Very much
so. Vince says, How excited? Robinson says, Do I have to spell
it out? Vince says, Don't tell me you're telling me Gina and the
big black male, dog or not, something is transpiring on the back
seat?! Robinson says, Detective. Vince says, I assume the dog did
not exit on his own at The Yale Club, but continued with Miss
Rendonello—and of course the driver. Am I right? Robinson says,
Blackie had no interest in exiting. Robinson proceeds to tell Vince
the details of the dog's transference at La Guardia into Gina's

keeping. Vince says, The dog was on the verge of being put down? Who are the animals who would do such a thing? She rescued him from certain death? Robinson says, Yes. (*Vince excuses himself, goes to Marie Rose, says, "A dog." Thinking what I'm thinking? She replies, Get back in there and choke out the details of the conversation in the limo.*)

Robinson says, He was a gentle dog. He was a happy dog. He was a loving dog. He had a hard on. Blackie turned in Gina's lap and licked the back of the driver's neck as the driver drove. Which the driver, Angelo, didn't appreciate. Vince says, What did Angelo say? He said, Jesus Christ, Gina! Vince says, Let's move on from the dog, shall we? Robinson says, Not so fast, detective. Eliot asks Gina who is going to care for Jackie when you're out of town. Likely three days a week in distant cities? Robinson says that Gina says, In this town? We have people their full-time work is dog walking, dog petting, dog sitting. Thirty dollars an hour or any fraction thereof, Gina stated. This is New York, boys, where anything is possible. No need of any kind goes unmet in this town, Gina said. Vince says, Which is what keeps people like me busy 24/7.

Robinson says, Actually, Detective Ventura, there wasn't much conversation in the limo. Vince says, Nothing outside dog talk? Robinson says, Not totally nothing. The driver many times said x-rated words when drivers cut him off or tailgated. I think Conte said, So kind of you, Gina, to take us into the city that never sleeps. Gina said back, My pleasure.

Robinson says, Then I changed the subject. I said, Does that jerk Captain Kidd bother you much? A lot? Make undesired moves in your direction? Gina said, All of the above, but I give it back to him on the chin. Conte says, Does it make him back off when you give it to him on the chin? She says, Never. Then I say to Gina, Gina, maybe someone should take a hammer to his knee-caps. She says, Eventually. (*Vince notes "eventually."*) Robinson says, Then I say, does Big Frank know about this harasser in your life? In close quarters in the cockpit? She says, No, Mr. Robinson.

So I say, No one knows but me and Eliot? She says, By the way, when we were close to landing another plane was on our runway. Which is why we pulled up so steeply or else catastrophe. Conte says, Well, at least Captain Kidd gets credit for *that*. She said, He was on his phone. I took over. Then Conte said, On his phone during the final approach? Yes, she said, surfing porn. Excited. Then Robinson says, What an a-hole. No one knows about his abusive habits but me and Eliot? She answered, Someone knows who cares very much. Who loves me. (*Vince takes note.*) Vince says, Did she identify this person? Who totally loves her like a boyfriend? Robinson says, Not to the best of my knowledge. Her vibe wasn't giving off boyfriend. Vince looks up from his legal pad, says nothing, thinking: *When in this room they say that b.s. about their recollection, they're holding back.*

Vince says, Anything else, Chief, no matter how unimportant? Oh, Robinson says, just personal stuff. She doesn't see much of her father, who is consumed 16 hours a day. She's away too much herself. Relatives far away. Just personal stuff. Strictly. Unhappy feelings. Lonely for family. Vince, *with urgency*, says, Relatives or *a* relative far away? Robinson says, I admire your hunger for detail. You're a heckava detective, detective. A detail like that with Blackie always with his paw out to me? Who can recall?

Vince says, Anything else? Robinson says, A lot of silence on the 30-minute drive except when Jackie a.k.a. Blackie wasn't getting stroked. Which is when he starts whimpering and she says something about love. According to Gina, most humans can't be trusted with love. You can give it, they often give you nothing, said Gina, but a dog gives and gives even when you don't give, Gina said she heard it said from a relative. (*Vince notes: love dog relative.*) In the love and trust department, dogs are superior to humans, Gina said. Vince wants to know who in the family she heard the philosophy of dog-love from. Robinson says, She didn't specify a name. Vince says, Might she possibly have said "uncle?" Robinson says, Maybe, maybe not. What she did say was, I can't keep this sexy beast long term. He needs a permanent home with an owner who'll give him perfect love until the day Blackie passes. So I say to her, How do you go about finding an angel? She says, Sometimes an angel flies in through the window. Like a poem, she says.

Okay Detective Ventura? Can't offer you anything more. Vince says, You've given me more than you know. Stay well, Chief Robinson. Stay safe.

5

Having gone that morning on separate ways, Conte and Robinson meet at noon at The Yale Club, where they are promptly seated in the Tap Room by *maître d'* Arturo Zapata, he of commanding elegance, to whom Conte poses this mischievous question: Sir, Conte says, have you seen the movie *Zapata!*? Starring Marlon Brando? In the title role as the revolutionary Emiliano Zapata? Arturo Zapata replies that he has seen the *film* (he never says *movie*) twice—finding it a "touch tedious" on first "screening" and "cliché-driven" on the second. Conte asks Arturo Zapata if he has ever been called "Marlon." Arturo says, By my wife, many times, when she has unspecified wishes. It is unnecessary for her to specify. It is only necessary for her to say Marlon. He adds, As an artist Mr. Brando—if I may opine—is quite good, as usual. Of course. But he does not touch the level of the unforgettable Gwyneth—whose last name I forget. He departs.

A coke for Robinson. A double Johnnie Walker Black for Conte. They butter their popovers. They order the black bean soup for reasons neither wishes to discuss, especially at the lunch table. Robinson says, I hope you're in control of that hard stuff. Conte says, The point, brother, is to lose it. Robinson says, You're starting to scare me, El. I don't know what to say anymore.

Robinson looks up to the ceiling of the Tap Room. He says, Coffered. What, says Conte? Robinson says, Coffered. A word I learned in Art History 101. The ceiling—it's coffered. We had to define technical terms in 25 words or less for the final exam. Which I Ace-ed. *Contrapposto.* My favorite word, which I liked to perform in the isolation of my dorm room. *Contrapposto.*

Meaning, Conte says? When we used to ask the prof to define a word, Robinson says, he'd go: LOOK IT UP! Conte says, Give me a hint, Robby. Robby says, Just looking at the ceiling. Just looking at the gleaming hard wood floors. The breath-taking length of the bar. I sit here and feel accepted in the upper reaches of WASP America. I feel good. Conte says, What did they spike your Coke with? You losing control? Robinson says, I feel good. In this place, El. This—this Yale Club. Three restaurants including one at the top on the twenty-second floor, with big windows, big views. The Chrysler Building looming. I scoped the library. Peace and tranquility in there as people read and tap on their laptops. The fragrance of old books. How quiet in there with restrooms so clean and aromatic behind the stacks. They have here a workout room of size with machines and a squash court. The Lounge. The Lounge, El. What can anyone say about the Lounge extravagant enough to honor the Lounge? The people who work here. Where do they find them so nice? Such kindness constantly shown. Such good cheer. There's everything here that a person could ever want, because you could live here without having to step outside into the noise and the pollution, the human density of the real world. The f-ing real world. Because this place is a total world—to live and die at The Yale Club. Happily ever after.

Conte says, Tell me the truth. What's troubling you? Robinson says, Look who's talking. I see you here, but you're not really here. Maybe you need another bowl of this soup. To get you relieved back into the present. Conte says, Yeah.

Robinson says, By any chance did you see the *New York Times* this morning? Conte says, I don't read that holier-than-thou rag. I thought things would change when they hired a black Executive Editor. Turns out this guy's whiter than a… whatever. Robinson says, So you didn't see the front-page story about this guy from New Rochelle, who came down with this Chinese thing happening in Seattle? So this guy takes the commuter train loaded with people from New Rochelle, densely packed, El, to go to work here at his law firm, which is an f-ing stone's throw from where we sit. It's in the *Times*. This contagion in Seattle is over the top contagious. Conte says, It couldn't have jumped over the entire continent in one leap and landed in New Rochelle. Is the *Times* that hysterical with fake news? Robinson says, They think he caught it at a bat mitzvah in New Rochelle. Or brought it in there. Conte says, So this is now a Chinese-Jewish thing? This guy a Chinese Jew? Robinson says, Are we surprised? So depending how contagious this thing is, which is the worry, according to the *Times*, there could be a lot of cases here, soon. Thank God, El, The Yale Club of New York City is not in New Rochelle. Here's the thing, El. This guy is not the first case in New York, according to the *Times*. He's number 2. The first is some woman who went to Iran, where they have it in spades. Conte says, Did this guy have an intimate relationship with this Iranian? Robinson says, She *went* to Iran, El. She is not *herself* an Iranian. If she was deeply intimate with the Chinese Jew, the two of them are keeping it to themselves in order to protect their respective spouses and children from hearing in the media that their parents are extra-marital disease vectors. A lot of people attended that bat mitzvah, hundreds, at the most popular synagogue in New Rochelle. He possibly injected the entire synagogue and those hundreds went out and injected hundreds more, not to mention friendly Christian onlookers in the vicinity of the synagogue, who are described in some quarters as Jew-lovers, who themselves become disease vectors in heavy numbers. Conte says, I feel terror on behalf of the Jews. Everything said forever about these people, dirty Jews, as it is traditionally phrased among the Christ-lovers, whose term for "Jew" is "Christ-killer." *Mazza Cristo*, as the worst Italians I grew up with used to say. If this Chinese thing carpet bombs America, a second holocaust is on the menu.

Conte, the grim-faced, is laughing. He says, A Chinese Jew? You cannot be serious. The guy is no doubt a Jew, unless he was one of the drooling Christian onlookers at the synagogue. Which I doubt. He is unlikely Chinese as well as Jewish. Imagine the odds of that in New Rochelle! The *flu*, Robby, is Chinese. The

Chinese flu is what it is called at high levels of our government. They say that bats in China are eaten for lunch. This is how it started. Lunch in China.

Conte and Robinson fail to suppress their fits of giggling, as people at nearby tables shoot them furtive glances. Conte and Robinson, after rough mornings, are glad to be in each other's company, sixty-five years of good company, both believing (though not yet having shared the belief) that not many more years remain. Robinson says, This thing that's hitting Seattle is going to be a big topic on *Saturday Night Live*. Mass Death: A Comedy. El, they said that this so-called Chinese Jew of New Rochelle has an office very near Grand Central Station, which I don't need to remind you is right across the street. Next to Grand Central, you noticed, how could you not, that big office building? He probably came there in the last few days sicker than a dog, infecting everything in sight, including the water coolers. Especially the water coolers. Who knows if this miserable mother went to Yale? Had a leisurely lunch in this room as he shed the virus. Possibly at this table we're sitting at. Robby, Conte says, pull back. You're at the edge.

Robinson says, Okay, then, El. So how was your morning at the Museum of Modern Art? Conte says, I didn't go. I made a second visit to the producer. Robinson says, You're kidding. I told him, Robby, I wasn't speaking hyperbolically when I told him yesterday that I'd move him from the surface of the earth to a dark and private place underneath if he tried something with Catherine. Robinson says, Again you threatened his life? A serious crime which Detective Ventura has no interest in, lucky for you, in pursuing at the moment. Conte says, You said you were going to take a long stroll in Central Park, but you somehow ended up at the 17th Street Station? Don't tell me long stroll. We don't do that anymore. Robinson says, You left this place and were on your way supposedly to the Museum, to the third floor where you wanted to surround yourself with abstract expressionism, whatever that is, you could explain it to me. You look at something and you see nothing you've ever seen in the world. Am I right? Yes, Conte says, it's a pleasure to leave the world. Robinson says, Death before death? Conte says, Nice. Robinson says, I come down to the lobby, Jade spots me, motions me over. A uniformed cop is at the counter talking to her. She says to me, This nice officer would like to speak to you. The officer asks me if I would do Detective Ventura at the 17th a favor, which I'm not under obligation to do, and accompany him to the 17th because Ventura wants to have an informal chat. I don't say I've been in law enforcement forever and I know "informal" means something serious will be on the table that involves me. Long story short, this Ventura knew all about what you did yesterday at the producer's office. He'll no doubt hear again from the producer what you did again this morning, probably already got the word.

Conte says, So what's the deal? Robinson says, He's exclusively interested in the girl, Gina Rendonello, and what we may have gathered from her, on the ride from La Guardia, about her uncle. Conte says, You mean Big Frank, don't you, her father? No, I mean her *uncle*, El, who is none other than Jimmy Red Rendonello, the New York version of Boston's Whitey Bulger, only worse, if that can be imagined. It's a strong belief in law enforcement circles for years that Gina is Red's favorite person and vice-versa. So thanks to you and the complaint they got at the 17th from this producer, Ventura has an excuse to question Gina about where her underground uncle might be. Ventura never said that right out, but that's what I put together. Conte says, Why not go straight to Gina? Robinson says, My guess? He wants to tighten the noose by getting testimony from us that compromises her. If Ventura can pin her with a charge of foreknowledge as to Red's whereabouts, then he can get her to spill the beans and bring this manhunt to a conclusion. But he'll never flip her. Because these involved Italians—no disrespect to your people, El—they are as bad as the involved Irish, like Whitey Bulger's family. They don't break because they don't believe there's any such thing as the larger social good. They don't accept that society exists. For these people, the only good is their family and everybody else can go to hell and they'll help them get there. Conte says, Will Ventura be interviewing me, you think? El, does the bear do s– wherever it wants to?

Conte says, It's on the menu. What, says Robinson? Conte says, Prune juice. A large glass for me. How about you? Robinson says, Sooner the better.

6

After lunch, in the Lounge: Conte, who despises the *New York Times*, reads the *New York Times*. So much the better to feed his bottomless capacity for aggravation. Robinson, seeking reality at garish and scandalous levels, reads the *New York Post*. Another Coke for Robinson, another Johnnie Walker Black for Conte, who mutters, as he reads, an elaborate obscenity. Robinson says, Hey. Don't let that rag give you an ulcer. This, he says, holding up the *Post*, puts you in touch with an enhanced life.

They read again, Conte quietly seething, Robinson in tranquility until he raises his eyebrows and says, My God, El! That pilot? Conte says, Don't tell me that jerk made the news. Robinson says, Oh yeah. Listen to this:

Outside his East 10th Street apartment, across from Tompkins Square Park, Captain Jon W. Kidd of Delta Airlines was found face down on the sidewalk by a neighbor at 2:45 a.m. Preliminary on site forensic analysis determines cause of death as manual strangulation, with bare hands, along with shocking severance of tongue. Robbery as motive is ruled out as wallet, diamond ring, watch, and three gold neck chains were found undisturbed on the victim's lifeless body. Our source at department headquarters informs us that the wallet contained four one hundred dollar bills. At this time, police comb the neighborhood for potential witnesses and urge any who may have happened to be passing through at the hour of the unfortunate tragedy to come forward. Anonymity guaranteed.

Conte says, He was an asshole. Robinson says, He was an asshole, but keep in mind he made a complaint to the airport police at La Guardia. We're going to be questioned. Including the girl. Who he constantly harassed with verbal implications. Conte says, Verbal, physical. In this era, no difference. If Gina did it, she'll become a feminist icon. But I don't believe she could've. He was fit and young. With her bare hands? No. Cut out his tongue? Never.

Robinson says, Whoever did this murder left a message. Conte says, Symbolic message? The severed tongue. Who does this kind of thing? Robinson says, As a pilot, if he had regular routes to Miami, El Paso, Tucson he was in a position, if he was dirty, to transport contraband on behalf of cartels. He was an arrogant little bastard, this we know, who maybe tried to hold the boys up for a better cut—made a stupid threat to expose. Conte says, Hence: the symbolic tongue removal. If the asshole was involved.

Conte says, If we were investigating, that'd be a possibility we'd have to explore. Speaking of mysteries, where were you last night? Tompkins Square Park at East 10th? It was after 3 when you got in.

Robinson says, I tip-toed in and should've known you were awake when you all of a sudden stopped snoring. Conte says, So where were you if not on the Lower East Side cutting off Kidd's tongue? Robinson says, Upper West Side, 103rd Street and West End Avenue. Conte says, You know someone up there? Robinson says, A white woman who was the cause of my miserable marriage and the children who treat me like garbage, thanks to their mother who belonged in the morgue from day one. Who you knew well. I married black. She—the white woman on the Upper West Side—married a white man after a year and a half with me that couldn't be improved. Not even in Heaven, she used to say. She left Utica the night after we made love for the last time. No letter of goodbye. Two years later she tells a mutual friend to tell me that she had to marry within her race. She disappeared in the dead of winter. Without a word. My sister who's savvy with Facebook found her location a month ago and told me that her husband died a year ago. Which is why when you offered to come down here free of charge, thanks to Dr. Gallatin, I took you up.

103rd at West End Avenue. That's where I was for several hours last night. Several satisfying hours.

Conte says, You re-heated the passions of yesteryear? Robinson says, No. Don't make fun of me, brother. You came to New York to scare the producer—which you did. I came to New York to scare her. To punish her, which was my secret purpose. She has to pay for destroying my life. Conte says, Did you make her pay? Robinson says, I did and she will. Until she croaks.

Conte is about to ask how so when Akash approaches saying, Sorry to intrude, gentlemen. I have received a call from the front desk inquiring if Mr. Conte might be here. When I answered in the affirmative, I was asked to inform you Mr. Conte that Dmitri at the front desk wishes to see you, as soon as possible. Robinson says, Dmitri, not Jade? Akash says, Unfortunately, Jade has been taken ill and driven home. Conte says, Is it serious? Akash says, I cannot say. It would not be correct to say. Fever. I should not be revealing such details. Dmitri awaits you, Mr. Conte, with an officer of the law who communicates through Dmitri that you must have no concerns. It is said to be routine.

Robinson says, as Akash leaves, Ventura. No doubt wants to quiz you about what was said in the limo. I like Gina. Conte says, So do I. Robinson says, Let's protect her from Ventura's velvet claws.

* * *

In advance of the Conte interview, Vince Ventura actually resisted his wife's directive and did not replace his spectacle of sweets by dispatching a cruiser all the way up to the Bronx's Little Italy. Because much closer to the 17th Precinct (51st east of Lexington) there it is, at 11th and 1st Avenue: Veniero's, founded in 1894 and the equivalent under one roof, Vince tells Marie Rose, of all Arthur Avenue pastry shops. She, Marie Rose, who had never been there—unlike Vince, Vince's father, Vince's father's father— had to see for her skeptical self. The trays she brought back were a temptation irresistible even to those beset by severe diabetes. Marie Rose says, You were right, lover. Be on your toes with this Conte. I can't be here to monitor. He says, How come? It's today? The doctor for female troubles? Hope to God, Marie—She says, No troubles. Routine. Stay on your toes with this guy.

Vince greets him and assures him that he is not a person of interest, except no doubt to your wife, Mr. Conte. Conte says, I better be.

Vince is shaken by Conte's appearance. He works to keep his eyes averted. Conte sees Ventura's discomfort and says, Recent open-heart, six hours on the table. Vince says, No kidding! You look normal to me. Conte says, Don't bullshit me, Detective. I know what I look like and I know you know about my first conversation with the producer. I know because Antonio Robinson told me. You don't care about that. Which I also know. Would you care if I did a second verbal assault? This morning? Which I did? Vince says, I already know. The pig called in again. This report here (tapping finger on a sheet of paper) quotes you as follows: "I'll disembowel you, inch by inch, and feed it to my pet vulture. Inch by fuckin' inch." You have an actual pet vulture? Which you brought to New York in an airplane? Conte says, I don't have a pet vulture. Vince says, We could be very good friends. Listen. I don't care, though my bosses might. People say crazy things they don't act on. I'm chasing someone else. Conte says, Who is it? Vince says, Do you know the name James Red Rendonello? Conte says, Vaguely. I don't follow the annals of crime, as Antonio does. Or my wife. I'm no longer fascinated by these animals.

Vince says, Robinson didn't tell you what we talked about? Conte says, Sure. More or less Gina and her love of dogs and the one she had in her lap. Ventura says, What specifically about the dog? Conte says, Some concern which I didn't quite get about taking care of him. Something about love. I didn't quite hear it clearly. Vince says, Too bad for me that you couldn't.

Conte says, Let me tell you about my ears. My hearing has been going south for several years. I bought deluxe hearing aids, which I don't like to wear. They amplify ambient noise. They sometimes cause an itch which you can't itch unless you take them out. Imagine doing that at a restaurant or on the john. They pick up ear gunk and need to be cleaned, which takes skill to take them apart, which I don't have. I could learn. Sure. But I don't want to learn. I learned to drive a car, once, more or less. I'd rather not. That's as far as I go with mechanical things. The car. The batteries go every 5 days. I am able to change them, barely. These are the general shortcomings of hearing aids and myself as an aids user. When I boarded the plane to Syracuse I didn't have them in for fear they'd react with a will of their own inside my head and damage my brain, as we ascended and descended. I never put them back in since we got to this city. So I didn't have them on in the limo. A blessing. Because when you have ears like mine ambient sound is amplified with or without hearing aids. In the limo, the tires turning at high speed on the road. You have no idea how that sounds until you have ear failure. Not to mention cars passing on either side of you. I had trouble picking up the conversation in the limo. People who have ear failure, who are not wearing their aids? They do a lot of nodding, to pretend they hear you. It's quiet in here. I hear you well except the coffee pot is perking and it irritates me. Would you like to turn it off? God forbid you have your aids in and go into the shower with them in. Six grand down the toilet and electroshock in the head. Possible brain damage. I know. I went into the shower once with them in. I sustained brain damage. The pair of aids I brought to this city is my second pair. Okay? By the way, never go to bed with them in. Unless you're a back-sleeper, you crush them. They tell you to insert them first thing in the morning. For breakfast. But I don't. Because breakfast conversation? There a Men's Room, close by I hope? Real close?

When Conte rises to visit the Men's Room, he does so with a tightened face and a furrowed brow. When he returns, it is with the face of a man experiencing indescribable relaxation. He says, I doubt I have anything of interest for you, Detective. I do have one question, though, for *you*. How is it that you knew of Robinson and me and where we were staying? Ventura says, You made it easy. When the producer's receptionist asked how she should identify you for her boss, you told her you were an old friend just in town for a few days and staying at The Yale Club.

Please stay a little longer, Mr. Conte. Correct me if I am wrong. You are a Melville expert? Hiram Melville? Conte, amused, does not correct him. He says, You are not wrong. Ventura says, You wrote a book on that guy and I am thinking your sensitivity to literature makes you yourself very sensitive to the silent nuances of a person's personality. What a person might be like without that particular person saying much in a lot of words. You're a literary man. I'm asking you to do me one favor before you leave. I need your impressions, your "reading," as you literary people say, of Gina Rendonello. What's she like, humanly speaking? What is she capable of when out of view?

Conte says, You think she's the missing link, more than her father would be? To Uncle Jimmy? Ventura says, The word is that the uncle and Big Frank never got along. Which is why—Conte jumps in, You believe she's the key to the uncle's whereabouts? Vince says, Absolutely. Conte says, You want a psychological profile? Vince says, Absolutely. Conte says, Talk to the FBI. Vince says, I'm talking to you. Conte says, We need to start from the outside in. Vince says, I'm all ears. Conte says, Tall like a model. Beautiful, unlike most models. Fit, strong looking. Unlike all models. A warmth in her beauty. Not stuck on herself. A welcoming beauty. From what I observed of her interaction with the Captain, she fears nobody. Especially not men with authority over her. Like the Captain. Vince wants to know if she spoke about the Captain in the limo. Conte says, From what I could hear, no. She spoke about and to the dog. Vince says, Possibly who he'd end up living with? Conte stares blankly. Vince says, Doing my job. Crossing all the I's and dotting the T's.

Conte says, I wasn't with her long, but I think she'd be easy to be with on a long term basis. Easy to like. Easy to snuggle up to. Vince says, Think she's capable of violence? Conte says, Like her uncle, you mean? Vince says, I wasn't thinking of him, I was thinking of something else, but sure, that too. Conte says, People like you in law enforcement know most of us are capable, but don't do it. People like you know that the wimpiest guy out there, the gentle types in general—they sometimes do the worst acts—like the wimp in Utica who raped a 10-year-old Asian girl and hanged her from a tree in the public park. When he was picked up and questioned he said he couldn't have done it in the time frame they were indicating because in that 4-hour frame he was at an adult store watching pornography for 4 hours. Gina? No. At the same time, who really knows? I think she's a good person. A generous person. No. I don't accept the thought that she could've killed Captain Kidd. Which is the elephant in the room we haven't addressed. Vince says, Which is being investigated downtown.

Conte says, That writer, Hiram Melville? He wrote about a man obsessed with a White Whale. Vince says, Jimmy Rendonello is a red head. Conte says, Be careful, Detective Ventura. The man who maniacally chased the White Whale was destroyed by the White Whale. Vince says, I read your book. Ahab's problem was that he didn't have a wife to rein him in, named Marie Rose. I intend to harpoon Red Rendonello. See him spout black blood.

Walking back to The Yale Club from the 17th Precinct Station in the finest drizzle, without an umbrella, Eliot Conte sees an expensively-dressed, middle-aged black male, also without an umbrella, wearing a blue surgical mask, tight-fitting blue surgical gloves, and the blue booties required of all personnel in the O.R. Conte thinks, An elegant kind of nut job. Because this is New York. Wouldn't be surprised if he's wearing a blue condom.

The man walks ahead of Conte, all the way to 50 Vanderbilt, where he turns into The Yale Club of New York City.

7

They sit alone, drunk, at 10 p.m. in the Lounge. The large wedding party of recent Yale graduates—all those vivid Yalies, all departed. Conte says, Who, Robby, has the richer chemical life? I take 11 medications, daily. You 7. Those Yalies? Zero. Their sculpted bodies. Their heads thrown violently back in laughter. A wonder they don't break their necks in joy. I hope they live forever. I really do. Notice the black girl with pink strands of hair? The white guy in a tux with dreadlocks? Robby says, Question is, What did those *Yalies* see? You want me to tell you? No, Robby. I'm telling you anyway. Two guys on their way out. They see us for one, one-thousandth of a second—they tremble for one ten-thousandth of a second. Let's have six more drinks.

Conte says, Let's change the subject. Robinson says, Because you fear the subject? Conte says, What's the subject I'm afraid of, but you're not? Robinson says, Who says I'm not afraid of the subject, old man? Conte says, What was her name? Who you made pay last night? And somehow for the rest of her life? Robinson says, Melody. Conte wants the story. Robinson says, In Syracuse, at security, they didn't object to it—what I had in my carry-on. Conte says, What didn't they object to in your carry-on, old man? Robinson says, The container of liquid shoe polish.

* * *

As Angel Rodriquez enters Ventura's lair, sirens hard south on Lexington and Third Avenues, penetrating with ease the walls of the 17th. What Angel sees: Ventura in a close-fitting, Navy blue

pinstriped suit, black tie, pale blue shirt and silver cuff links. An
orange scarf draped over his shoulders. Hair slicked back, clean
shaven, aroma of cologne. Ventura's right hand slowly and cease-
lessly rotating a wedding band. Cell phone at the ready. What
Ventura sees: a man in his early thirties, medium height in ol-
ive-colored cargo pants, jean-jacket, white T-shirt showing NYC
PLAYERS stretched tight across a chest bursting with much
iron-pumping. Fashionable 3-day stubble. Shaved head.

Ventura, rising, saying nothing, motions him to a chair. Angel
sits and Ventura proceeds in a monotone to unleash his mad welcome: St. Peter's etcetera.

Rodriguez says, I don't give a shit about St. Peter's, the
Yankees—don't call me A-Rod. Don't call me—the bar area at
the Waldorf is what? Like what? What the—you believe in God?
Really? You want to talk about Gina Rendonello? That's what
this is all about, right? To get to the uncle? That's what's on your
mind? Red Rendo—am I right? Sometimes I lose my fuckin' tem-
per. Too many fuckin' times. No offense, detective. Great fuckin'
suit, detective. Great ensemble.

Ventura looks away. He's in the room, but he's not in the
room. His Secretary of State is not on the other side of the one-
way window. Tests. He's cold. She's undergoing tests. Wraps the
orange scarf—it's actually hers, confiscated long ago, she never
complained—snugly around his neck. He turns to Rodriguez who
thinks, This guy is in trouble. Or an act to get me to drop my
guard, say things I'll never say.

Ventura says, Good of you to come. You didn't have to. Sorry
about what I laid on you, The Waldorf, so forth. Mr. Rodriguez,
I've never been a clever detective, the kind you read about in detective novels. You read detective novels? Rodriguez says, I don't
read novels. Ventura says, Those are not real detectives in those
detective novels. I'm real, maybe. You drove Miss Rendonello,
two guys, and a dog from La Guardia. This I know. It's the dog,
not Miss Rendonello, who interests me. You were seen driving
off from The Yale Club, with the girl and a black dog in the back

seat. Rodriguez says, What's with the "I was seen?" That how you people talk to suspects of a crime? What am I suspected of? Ventura says, Sorry. Old habit. You are not suspected of anything. Except blunt honesty. Rodriquez says, Trying to get on my good side? Ventura says, You drove Miss Rendonello and the black dog to her condo at The Royal York? 420 East 64th? Rodriguez says, You ask me questions you know the answer? What's the point? Ventura says, Just plodding along. I'm just a plodder. Can I get you a cup of coffee? It's actually good. Rodriguez says, I don't take caffeine in any form. Including chocolate. No nicotine, if you want to know. Ventura says, Never smoked? Rodriguez says, No. Ventura says, In my neighborhood we started young. I was 12. Stupid. You resisted the stupidity. Rodriguez says, How did you know the dog was black? Ventura smiles a little. Rodriguez says, Never mind. You talked to those two geezers from Utica. Obviously. Ventura says, Chauffeur's license. Yes? Rodriguez says, Naturally. Been driving a limo for a long time? Rodriguez says, Nine years. For Frank Rendonello, mainly. Until his daughter became a Delta pilot. Vince says, You drive exclusively for her? Angel says, No. Still mainly for Big Frank, but on his order I carry her to La Guardia, JFK, Newark, back and forth, 2-3 times a week.

A long pause. Ventura picks up phone. Taps it. Stares. Puts it down. He says, This dog will need dog food. A dog that size needs—who'll take care of him when she's gone half the week? You? You wouldn't mind, my guess? Or one of those people who walk dogs and scoop up their poop for a living? Or possibly a relative nearby who's nuts for dogs? Who won't charge an eye and a leg?

Rodriguez says, There's this old TV show you remind me of about a detective. It was called Columbus. You remind me of that show. The actor, I'm referring. What was that actor's name? Peter something. Peter Lorre! That's it! You know that show you remind me of? Vince says, *Columbo*. It was *Columbo*. Not Peter Lorre. Peter Lawford, I think. Or maybe Peter Ustinov. Anyway, Rodriquez says, like Columbo you come at things sideways. You give the impression you're out to lunch, then all of a sudden you eat their lunch. Ventura says, I'm married. To a woman, by the way. These days that has to be specified. Not that I—do you care about this issue of the gender of the spouse? Rodriguez says, No skin off my back. Ventura says, Or mine. Every day, Mr. Rodriguez, more sirens. Sirens and silence. More silence than I ever heard in the city that never sleeps. Whoever hears birds in this town? Sirens and birds. Miss Rendonello has a condo on the 9th floor. Facing south. Window facing south. You knew that? Rodriquez says, I helped bring her luggage and the dog up there. Ventura says, What was it like? Rodriguez says, Expensive. An expensive dream. Ventura says, You wouldn't mind living there in your dream? Rodriguez says, What's that supposed to mean? Ventura says, My dream too, with my female spouse. Rodriguez says, You worried about your wife?

* * *

—Liquid shoe polish
—Yep. Black.
—Something to do with making Melody pay?
—Saw it on her face when I arrived. Where has he gone? My beautiful boy? She says, Antonio, I never stopped loving you.
—Were you shocked after what? 50 years? How could you not be?
—Skin and bones moving hunched over with a walker. In other words—
—She was helpless. You could do what you wanted to her. With her.
—With her? Don't make me vomit. To her? Yes. Yet…
—Yet what?
—Something else.
—What?
—Forget it.

* * *

At The Royal York: Her condo: One million dollars. Of course, she couldn't afford it. Or the one-bedroom on the 13ᵗʰ floor: 750,000 dollars. Both bought for her by Big Frank—and put in her name.

The Royal York: a massive double building. 494 units. Too many faces to remember. That was the attraction. That's why she decided on The Royal York. Concierge. Gym. Doorman. Interior garden. Elevator. Pet friendly: That was also the attraction, pet friendly, though she had no pet and never contemplated acquiring one. Garage: Hasn't had a car in years. Her parking space is occupied by a silver Audi A8, California plate. Los Angeles area.

The Royal York, at East 64ᵗʰ, north side of the street, sitting between First and York Avenues. Running alongside York to its east, the FDR Drive, which hugs the East River. The River that is East. Between the FDR and the River, a trail stretching between Battery Park at Manhattan's southern tip to 125ᵗʰ Street. At 63ʳᵈ and York, a footbridge over the FDR down to the river trail. Walkers. Bikers. Runners. Dog walkers. The walkers, most, but not all, carry bags for poop removal and transportation.

She loves the muted gloss of the wide plank floors. The recessed lighting. The custom millwork. In this condo, she loves her isolation.

* * *

A ping from Ventura's cell. Marie Rose. He reads. Rises and goes to the window with his back to Rodriquez. Types response. Stands at window for what seems to Rodriguez like forever. Ventura returns to the table and says, So what sport do you play? Soccer or what you people call football? I grant. The true football. No hands. I admire. Can't see how it can be done. No hands. Rodriguez says, I don't play that sport or any sport. Ventura says, On your shirt. NYC PLAYERS. Rodriguez says, It's a theater company. In a way, I guess, a sport. Ventura says, You're an actor on the side, when you're not driving your limo? Rodriguez says, The writer and the director of the company, who's the same dude, he's the boss. His wife taught me years ago, English as a Second Language—she emails me out of the blue and says the boss needs someone to be a limo driver. Isn't that what you do, she says? Ventura says, English sounds like your first language. You were a great student. Rodriguez says, I like the flattery. So I say to her, I'm an actual limo driver, not an actor. She goes, Perfect. That's what he's looking for. Ventura says, You drove your limo on *stage*? Rodriguez says, I was on video with my limo. Ventura says, Did you have lines? Rodriguez says, Yeah. The boss says, Say what you would say to a passenger after the passenger is in and buckled up. So I go, Would you like a bottle of water? The boss says, Beautiful—how many times a week do you ask that question? I say, God knows. The boss says, So it is boring to say it? You're bored? You have no feelings when you say it? I say, Exactly. I summon no emotion. The boss says, I'm going to record you 100 times saying those words. 100. One of those times will be what I want. So we begin the recording, detective, and I say the words and he goes, Perfect on the first take. Ventura says, If you're in touch with the boss and he needs an actual detective, I—you married? I'm married. Did I already tell you that? Rodriguez says, Not married. After what I saw from my parents? Yeah. You already told me you were married. Ventura says, I'm at the age when you repeat yourself. My mind is starting to—you're in love with Gina? Rodriguez says, You're looking for a boyfriend which I'm not. Not her type. Ventura says, which saddens you. Rodriguez says, Do I have to sit here and—Ventura says, No. Leave. Leave if you want to leave. She got news from the cancer man I don't want to know. Rodriguez says, Who? Ventura says, My wife. Rodriguez says, You're better than Columbus. If the boss of that company needs a detective. Ventura says, She already had dog food at the condo? In anticipation of a dog? You had to go get it for her? Rodriguez says, The kind she wanted, which is the most healthy for dogs of all types and sizes, they sold it in New Rochelle—Royal Canin, she said she wanted.

But—Ventura says, Right. The National Guard won't let anybody in or out of there. They call it a hot spot. Let those people keep it in New Rochelle because we don't want them anywhere except up there in New Rochelle where they started it. Rodriguez says, It's all over the 5 boroughs, my opinion, we just don't know it. Ventura says, Did you get the proper dog food? Rodriguez says, An outlet in Hoboken. Ventura says, Which you brought back to her—how late was it? Rodriguez: 9 something. Almost 10. Ventura: You went up to her condo with a heavy bag, 9th floor? Rodriguez: 60 pounds. Yes. I went up there. Ventura: Did the big black dog greet you? Rodriguez: No. Did you hear him bark? No. Did you see him? No. No? Where was he, Mr. Rodriguez?

* * *

Melody's apartment, El, condo whatever. What's the word? Sordid? Fantastically sordid. Newspapers all over the floor. Empty beer cans galore. The odor. Fast food wrappers. Her money? She's living like this? Two cats and everything that goes with indoor cats? Overfull litter boxes. One in the kitchen. Dirty dishes piled high. The odor, I gagged.

—What was the first thing you did? Hug? Weep?
—I went over there with an idea, but on the spot I'm inspired by a new idea.
—The black liquid shoe polish goes on the back burner?
—I take pictures with my trusty cell. A ton of them.
—Of?
—The s- hole.
—Including her?
—She says don't. I say, Gonna stop me? Who's gonna stop me? She says, Please don't.
—Point of these pictures?
—They call it these days revenge porn. Onto the internet. In her name. Forwarded to her kids and grandkids.
—You have their contact info?

—You forget Chief of Police, me, with easy outreach to Federal sources?

—Then what?

—I read to her. The erotic letters, you wouldn't believe the graphic detail. She had writing talent. She sent them 3-4 times a week during our 18 months of romance at the university. She says, as I read, Oh, Antonio! I tell her eventually copies, 2 per week, to your kids and grandkids. All that fungus you spawned with the guy you married instead of me.

* * *

She's at home in Queens, in their narrow two storey, two bedroom, one bath, where they raised the twins who love their parents and call them three times per week from Chapel Hill and Chicago. Purchased 35 years ago with the joint wedding gift from her parents and his. Purchased "for peanuts," as Vince used to say—17,500—and now worth, as they say in the real estate game, "north of 400,000."

She gives Vince the news. They think they found something. Ovaries. Test next week would be definitive. Ultrasonography. Ultrasound. They insert a small probe.

Vince is sitting across from her at the kitchen table. He cannot speak or move to rise and put his arm around her. Something, he says? They found *something*? What something? They *think* they found? He reaches across the table and she puts her hand in his. Tumor maybe, Vince. Or cyst. Cyst isn't so, she says. Bad, he says? The other thing? Cancer, he says? Likely malig? Unclear, Vince. When, the test? A week from now, they hope. What? They *hope*? What do you mean, they *hope*? The hospitals they're saying are reaching a point. They're maybe going to be overwhelmed with this virus. They may cancel everything except immediate life and death situations. Vince: Isn't this? Marie Rose: Maybe not. If it is, Marie, it spreads. Why can't you have the test tomorrow? There's a schedule. I'm on it. Others ahead of me. Possible you won't get the test next week? Possible I won't. Who do I bribe? Like they do in Russia?

* * *

Akash informs them that he's about to close up. Would they like another before he does? They each request two more. They are very drunk, but do not slur their words, do not display fixed, stupid grins, or sad-sack self-pity They are stone drunks. More keenly focused than when they are sober. Agile fast-talkers. Coldly present. Conte says, Akash, wait, as Akash turns to go. Have you noticed how people say to oldsters like us, You look good? I mean oldsters in general. Not us in particular, of course, not us in particular. Akash is speechless. Robinson says, You look good—not to us in particular, of course—but they leave out "for your age." Because, Conte says, they are nice. They don't want to hurt the feelings of the old and deteriorated. The dying. For us in particular there are no words to describe our total descent. Since when, Akash, Robinson says, do you ever hear somebody say to a young person, You look good? Know why, Conte says, to the frozen Akash? Know why nobody says you look good to you and Jade? Because you and Jade always look good. Most young people tend to always look good. Even those who don't look good, they look good in comparison to us. Robinson says, The bastards! Robinson says, Speaking of good-looking, how's Jade doing, Akash? Talk to her like every night, how are you sweetheart so forth?

I have not.

How come?

She's in the hospital.

Visiting hours, Akash.

At her bedside, Holding hands, Akash.

Did you say, in the hospital? Why?

No talking. No visiting allowed. No contact. No visual. Nothing. She's in the hospital.

* * *

IN GINA'S CONDO

On dining room table: Hard copy of email from Delta inform-
ing her of the murder of Jonathan Kidd. Also print out of an
article from the *New York Post* describing the murder scene and
the wounds on the victim's body.

In her bedroom: a treadmill set at maximum speed. Gina not
walking (impossible) but running. 40 minutes. Shouting: Christ
Christ Christ.

Gina with two 10-pound free weights: Two sets of curls. 15
reps. Two sets of overhead presses. 15 reps.

Gina on her cell phone: Dialing, switching off before an-
swered. Dialing again: ditto. Dialing again: contact. "It's me."
Listening to a monologue. Shaking her head. Not responding.
Hand to forehead. Not speaking. Speaking: "Okay." Switches off.
Gina doing jumping jacks: 100. Christ Christ Christ.

Gina doing pushups as her cell rings: 25 pushups.

Gina checking phone message: Does not return call.

Gina doing a plank: 6 minutes with steady perfect form. No
sag of back. Very like a plank. Talking quietly throughout: Christ
Christ Christ. Very like a plank.

Gina with her supper. Untouched. Pasta Bolognese scraped
into the garbage disposal.

The 60-pound bag of dog food: Gone.

* * *

Akash has left. The lights in the Lounge are off except for the
small table lamp where they sit. A small round table. The face of
each—half illuminated, half in dark shadow.

Conte: I'm gonna, I'm gonna—

Robinson: You gonna what? You're drunker than—

C: I gonna say, I gonna tell you.

R: You gonna. I gonna. We all gonna—

C: Scream for ice cream.

R: You're drunker than Springtime.

C: Gayer than what? I forget.

R: Michael Jackson.

C: Dead, no? Dead creep?

R: Prejudiced about dead people?

C: Black dead people? MLK, Jr had big ones.

R: Yeah.

C: Yeah. I used to have 'em. Yeah.

R: Yeah. Spit it out, bro. What you gonna tell who

C: Old Italian joke. SSPP. *Serve solo per pisciare.* Good for pissing only.

R: Yeah.

C: You're a good man, Robby Brown.

R: Yeah.

C: Listen. That is not you. Kill. Self. Too.

R: Too? Who too?

C: Melody

R: She can't sing no more.

C: Needs you.

R: You nuts?

C: That is not you. Revenge-desire, kills on the inside. Heart destruction. High blood pressure. Eating binges. Look at your poundage. Forgive her.

R: She dropped me without a word.

C: Black white marriage then? Rare.

R: She married a white guy 3 weeks later. Two-timing her nigger.

C: Don't hurt her. Live now. Revenge, resentment, the past. Live. Choose the present, live or die.

R: I want her to suffer.

C: Take care of you and Melody. Life is good. Some of the time. Enough of the time. If you're lucky. You're not an asshole. Stop acting like one.

R: Father Conte, f-off. Look at yourself. That producer. Don't
    trust your wife?

C: What did you do with the shoe polish?

* * *

A cold day in the middle of March. 10:30 p.m. 44 degrees with
wind steady off the East River at 15 mph. Wind chill factor: near
freezing. A man in his early 60s, silver-haired at the sides, bald
on top. In white sweat pants, white running shoes, white T-shirt,
approaching the footbridge at 63rd and York. A small, one shoul-
der-strap backpack slung not at his back or side but at his right
chest. He's prepared for the night in an unusually quiet city.

He ascends the footbridge over the FDR. Reaching the top of
the curved structure, he halts, taking a deep breath, slowly exhal-
ing. Not shivering. Because he is not cold. Stretches calves, quads,
gluts. 20 deep squats. Facing the river now, arms thrust out wide
at his sides, like Pavarotti at the conclusion of a performance em-
bracing a wildly applauding audience, as screaming women throw
their panties at The Luminous Fat Man.

He descends over the FDR, down to the East River Trail.
He will not walk or jog. Tonight he will run north from 63rd to
125th—four miles at 8 minutes per mile. And back, same pace.
Then up over the footbridge—happy, in a full sweat—and a stroll
to 64th between York and 1st. Toward the building, 420 East 64th.
The Royal York.

At a window facing south on the ninth floor, a woman watches
him approach and enter. He takes the stairs to the 13th floor, rac-
ing two steps at a time.

8

19½ Pitt Street: The 7th Precinct Station, serving the Lower East Side, where Delta pilot Jon W. Kidd was found murdered at East 10th, opposite Tompkins Square Park, 2:45 a.m. The lead detective on the case is Mike Garcia—young (32), a rising star—and stymied. Forensic analysis has determined that the hands which choked Kidd to death and severed his tongue (nowhere to be found) were not gloved. Fingerprints on neck blurred. Useless. The search for the tongue was thorough. Stout-stomached men descended into sewers. Mike Garcia said to them human tongue is a delicacy. And the stout-stomached men blanched. Mike Garcia said that you guys didn't find the tongue because the killer ate it and soon the *Post*'ll baptize him The Tongue-Eater of the Lower East Side. And the stout-stomached men gagged, as Mike smiled.

Nothing under Kidd's fingernails of interest: No DNA-worthy fragments of the killer's skin as Kidd surely (surely?) struggled and clawed to save himself. A crime scene without a single trace of the killer. Extensive interviews conducted in the neighborhood were fruitless. No one, not even those awake at that hour, had seen or heard a thing. The insomniacs stayed in, reading, listening to music—earbuds affixed—consuming to no avail known soporifics, peanut butter and red wine. They did not go out for a stroll. Leave the apartment at that hour, officer? Encounter some sick animal and I don't mean a dog, officer? No, I do not walk after midnight. Ever. What was Jon Kidd, Garcia wanted to know, who did not own a dog, doing out at that time, a few steps from his apartment complex? Lured out? If so, how? Garcia will never know.

The case was ice cold as soon as Kidd was put on a slab, his corpse waiting to be claimed by his parents in Cleveland who feared to enter America's hottest hot spot of Covid-19. Garcia had nothing until—why not? Why not take seriously what the organization of young white collar guys, all African-American, had called in three days ago? Nothing to lose, they respect us, raise money for slain cops, give us tips—some of which have led to the solution of not-so-petty crimes.

So Mike Garcia called Nelson (Nellie) Reed, the leader of the organization, who had phoned the station to report a nut-job sighting on the night of the killing, at about the hour in question: An older, partially bald man, a vigorous ghost-runner all in white coming off the East River Trail in the shadows of the Williamsburg Bridge—a stone's throw or two from the Precinct Station—heading north through a zigzag of streets off the grid. Picked up by Devon at Houston, the runner continues north on Avenue D. Lost sight of but seen again 35 minutes later at 21st, followed on the trail by Rashid at a discreet distance to 37th, the U.N. area, where a gap in the Trail begins and closes at 60th. At 63rd the runner takes the footbridge down to York Avenue.

Nellie Reed tells Garcia that the runner was dressed in this "cold-ass weather" in sweat pants and a T-shirt, with something strapped to his chest. Nellie Reed tells Garcia that Cory picked him up on 63rd and York and followed him to a building at 420 East 64th. Garcia wants Nellie to know that he's grateful for what you guys do on behalf of the city, but have to wonder why your team would track this whacko all the way to 64th. Nellie replies, You know better than I do that solutions come from the boredom of work. From patience enduring through the boredom, sir. You know it well, Detective Garcia. This runner is likely just an innocent crazy dude. On the other hand—who at this point really knows? We put him in your good hands. Garcia asks if you guys want to be actual cops. Nellie says, Nah. We have good day jobs. At night, we look for legal adventure. You have guys, Garcia asks, positioned all along the eastern border? Just in *case*? Nellie says, Just like you, we're good at what we do.

Garcia locates the contact number for Kidd's frequent co-
pilot. The runner is a far-fetched possibility, at best. But Gina
Rendonello, though far-fetched too, needs to be interviewed.
Pointless, we plod along. Occasionally, at our best, we imagine.
Calls her cell several times, identifying himself, no response.
Rendonello, Rendonello. When he learns her address, he thinks,
life is weird, especially in this work. Hard police workers get lucky
sometimes. Mostly we don't. Chances this coincidence of ad-
dresses breaks the case? Unlikely.

* * *

Rendonello Rendonello. Related to? He contacts Delta Airlines
and passes on his request for an interview. Tells upper level executive, one level below Big Frank, that her failure to respond will
result in major embarrassment, I guarantee you, for Big Frank
himself. She calls. He tells her she needn't come to the station
on Pitt. He's happy to spare her that. Suggests meeting her at
The Royal York, if she likes. She wouldn't like, prefers a "neutral site" and names a diner on 2nd Avenue at 64th. Tomorrow, 3
p.m. The Chief of Security at La Guardia had alerted Garcia the
morning after the murder of the complaint lodged against her
by Kidd. Her phrase "neutral site" is lodged in Garcia's head. She
fears something?

* * *

Rendonello? *That* Rendonello? Related to the missing Rendonello
for how many years? Jimmy? Yes. Never any concern to Mike
Garcia. Red Alert, they called him, according to his older colleagues. Not even the tiniest of noises in the background of Mike's
work. Some obsessive, I'm told, in the 17th, his life work. Vince
Ventura, a name of casual ridicule in law enforcement among
older detectives. Who cares? The kind of guy, this Ventura, if he
breaks the most famous cold case in America, they make a movie,

a hero. Hot cases in the present, so many, what the tax payers pay for. Rendonello's underground for 16 years, where he hurts no one, no more. Why bother? Gina Rendonello: just another item on the list, to be checked off. In the end, a waste of time, but this is what we call our work.

* * *

At the diner. Garcia arrives through streets unusually deserted. Three patrons: an ancient Chinese male with glittering eyes and a Caucasian female, mid-teens, heavily tattooed. Why isn't she in school? Show her my badge. She'd tell me to fuck off. The third, a head-turning female, late 20s, early 30s. Must be Gina.

    Garcia: Ms. Rendonello? May I join you?

    Rendonello: Do I have a choice?

    G: I'd prefer to treat you to a drink and dinner, somewhere nice, while I don't grill you, while we lift a glass or two. (He has shocked himself. Can this be Garcia, the normally shy-around-pretty-woman guy?)

    R: Did they teach you that line in cop school?

    G: Couldn't help myself. Can I buy your coffee?

    R: The one I'm drinking?

    G: That one.

    R: You want to drink from my cup?

    G: Very much so.

    R: You can have it free of charge.

    G: The cup?

    R: My cup. What else?

    G: You tell me.

The waiter asks Garcia what he can bring him, as he deposits a glass of water. The waiter has a ring-pierced lower lip. Garcia looking away, says, Nothing, thanks. I'm having what she's having. The waiter says, So I'll bring you a coffee. Garcia says, No. What she's having now. The waiter says, A cup of coffee. Garcia says, No. Hers. Her cup. The waiter says, Whatever, and walks away.

G: You can drink something brought to you by that guy? The lower lip. Disgusting.

R: *Tu mi fai schivo* is the Italian for what you want to say to that guy, Detective. You disgust me, but the nuance of Italian is untranslatable: It implies you make me hawk up something spongy clinging to the back of my throat. *Schivo.* Say *schivo.*

G: *Schivo.*

R: Perfect. Like a Wop.

G: Is yours hot? Now?

R: My coffee?

G: That too.

R: This conversation is unrealistic. It's absurd.

G: Like love at first sight.

R: This is how, Detective Garcia, you get inside the defense of the shady types you need to squeeze info out of—with your obscene charm?

G: Yes. Inside.

R: *Bello.*

G: *Bello?*

R: Italian for handsome.

G: *Hermosa.*

R: What?

G: Spanish for beautiful. You.

R: Stop, detective. I have no idea where he is.

G: Who?

R: Don't play dumb. My uncle.

G: Who's talking about your uncle?

R: You are.

G: How old are you?

R: 33.

G: Me, 32. You, older woman. Etcetera.

R: Jimmy Rendonello. Red Rendonello. Red Alert. No idea where he is.

G: No interest. Zero. Believe me.

R: Just in me?

G: 100%

R: Get serious.

G: I'm serious.

R: Jon Kidd's murder?

G: Of course.

R: On the night of his murder, I was at home. From 6 p.m. until the next morning, when I flew out to Chicago. No. Of course not. No. There is no one who can verify my whereabouts between 6 p.m. and the morning after his murder. According to what I know, he was killed, from what I read, well after midnight. When I was in bed. Alone. "Verify my whereabouts." Isn't that how you dicks talk?

G: Yes. Gina. You didn't get along with this guy. He called in a complaint about you to La Guardia security. We know this. What's the story. Have to ask.

R: No story. His fragile ego. That's the story.

G: Let me say this: There's no way I think you did this. Hard to imagine a woman being able to pull off that kind of violence. Cutting off the tongue of insinuendos. Though I can't help but notice your hands. Wrists. Forearms. Formidable.

R: I do a lot of free weights.

G: At a gym?

R: At home.

G: He never came over? Uninvited? Doorman calls up, you say tell him to get lost?

R: No.

G: No contact whatsoever outside the job?

R: None. Except once in a West Village restaurant. I'm having dinner with a friend.

G: Boyfriend? Hope not.

R: Friend. Kidd winked. He mimed panting. Tongue out. Asshole of the first order. I'm sorry he got what he got. Awful. But do I honestly grieve? No.

G: Anything you can tell me about the asshole—with his tongue on display—that might shed light on the killing? An enemy? Not including you.

R: No.

G: Someone at The Royal York you told? About his behavior? A confidant?

R: Confidant?! What a word! No.

G: Anyone at all at The Royal York?

R: No.

G: Any chance that—

R: We could have dinner tonight?

G: I thought I was supposed to initiate.

R: Afraid of me?

G: A little.

R: Better that way.

G: For?

R: Guess.

G: Stop. You're unrealistic. Dinner at a place around here?

R: Yes. Wait. (She sends a text. From his vantage across the table Mike Garcia cannot read what she's writing, but is certain that at the end of the message she's hit the exclamation point a few times.)

R: Okay. Dinner at The Royal York.

G: A restaurant there on the first floor?

R: Ninth floor my condo. Let's go.

G: Early for dinner, no? 4 p.m.

R: Dinner at 6.

G: What'll we—

R: We'll do something. (They're walking to The Royal York. Sirens. Then silence more vehement than sirens.)

G: Law enforcement is getting the word. Get ready. They tell us, before the general public gets the word. Before it hits the fan. In a day or two, this city. All 5 boroughs. The Island. Many areas outside. Upstate. Jersey. All directions from Manhattan, the center of this nightmare. We're going into hard lockdown.

R: Lockdown? More specifically means?

G: Restaurants, bars, fast food joints, hair and nail salons, barbers of the old school—everything they deem nonessential. Closed. You will stay in your condo, Gina. Seeing nobody.

R: Grocery stores, surely—

G: Essential, yes. If you can afford it, they'll deliver to you.

R: People who can't afford it will lose a lot of weight.

G: Including the slim ones. Poor bastards.

R: Friends and lovers? How about friends and lovers?

G: Not part of your living quarters? No touching. Separated. No physical anything. Hospitals and cops—we'll be pressed to the limit and over. Airports—you might not be working for a long time. Trains, long range buses will basically shut themselves down. No passengers on city buses except for the lower classes who get infected on the buses. People will flock to car rentals—those who can afford it, but there'll be nothing left to rent. Trapped. Unless you have your own car and then you drive to your house in the country.

R: I don't have a car.

G: You could lean on me if you're in trouble. Would you?

R: In a heartbeat.

G: Trapped. This is what we hear. This is the word, Gina.

R: Separated friends and lovers? I have a spare toothbrush.

G: This is serious, Gina.

R: I am serious, Mike.

G: The level of death will be extreme. The level of suffering before death, they say, will be unspeakable. The ER will be unspeakable.

R: In the meanwhile, in the present, we're not suffering. A pasta in the present you wouldn't believe how good. To be consumed in the present. You won't suffer tonight, trust me.

G: Describe the unbelievable pasta.

R: I'll surprise you. Anticipation is good.

G: You surprise me.

R: This will be our—

G: First and maybe last date.

R: People living together—they don't date, do they, Mike?

9

In the Lounge again, 2:30, drinking heavily again. The Lounge flies of The Yale Club of New York City:

—You went back to see Melody this morning? To forgive her, that why? That's what you did. You forgave the lousy bitch, who ruined your life. You stopped living in the lousy past.

—I went back with it. Black. Liquid black.

—What did you do? What? Answer me.

—I painted black. Her face. Minstrel Melody.

—What did she do?

—She said, Let me. She takes the brush. She dips it, and she paints her forehead.

* * *

So Vince and Marie Rose waited, what else could they do? For the message from her gynecologist. What else could they do? Waiting to be told the surgery was on. Or not. Vince? Wait? To make love to his wife? Once more before the news hits—once more snuggled into her soft place. Marie Rose was eager. Afterward, after—he said, I don't want to say that word about myself. She said, In your case that word doesn't apply. Vince, the "i-word" doesn't apply. Don't even say it in your mind. He said, Marie Rose, how about your mind? Do you say it now in your mind?

* * *

The lobby of the Royal York. Gina and Mike approaching the elevators. Gina, about to press the "up" button, when the door opens and they step out—a man all in white, sweat pants, T-shirt, running shoes and, loosely leashed, a large black dog. Before he can shorten the leash and restrain him, the big black dog lurches toward Gina, whimpering, up on his hind legs in an actual embrace—front legs over her shoulders—dog and girl. Gina, holding him tightly, saying in a low voice, What's going on? Yes yes you're a good boy, yes you are.

* * *

Jade Miranda is on a ventilator. A misdiagnosis. Of course. She is too young to have it. Ventilators are for old people like Conte and Robinson.

* * *

Angel Rodriguez has no appetite. He's shivering in his bed. Seeing Al Capone approach with a baseball bat. Al Capone looking like, exactly like, Robert DeNiro.

* * *

—I painted, El. What did you do while I was gone?
—Answered questions from our friend Detective Ventura. Good guy. He said he heard something. Called because he wanted to help me out, "forewarn," he said. He would get a lawyer soon if he's standing on my shoes.
—Walking in your shoes?
—You are not a cruel person but you became one at our age? Ventura says they might arrest me for threatening the life of—
—She said, she says, Darling … Possibly arrested? We'd better get back to Utica … We all love you, Antonio, she said.

—Because cops here, Antonio, are not allowed to go to Utica, the crown jewel of upstate hinterlands.

* * *

Gina says to the man holding the leash, I just love dogs and they just love me. She laughs in a way that Garcia recognizes as the laugh of suspects, cornered, when he has them under harsh interrogation. Laughter of those with a secret. He notes that Gina does not look at the man holding the leash. Garcia bends down, squats, and the dog licks his face. Garcia laughs a genuine laugh and says, In this hard time this town is facing, friendliness is what we all need from all quarters. The isolation is going to kill our peace of mind. Pointing to Gina, he says, This is Gina Rendonello. I'm Mike Garcia (standing, thrusting out his hand). The man, concealing his hostility not quite perfectly, says, with a cold stare, Charlie Gasko. Does not shake Garcia's hand. Yanks the big black dog hard to the lobby exit.

* * *

Marie Rose comes to Vince's rescue. She says, More than ever, Vince, turn to Saint Jude, the big specialist in lost causes. Vince does not reply. Thinks, Lost causes? Patron Saint of Failed Penises, I pray to thee, restore my power in the sack.

The so-called failed lover turns instead to his work—plunging more deeply than ever into the strongest lead he's had in 16 years on Jimmy Rendonello. It's the Royal York. Gina is there. The dog is there. The dog food was delivered there. She can't take proper care of the dog. She's either hiring a dog sitter for her days away—or she's alerted her uncle, who loves dogs more than he's ever loved humans, including his parents, and he's eager to come back to his old stomping ground after 16 years from wherever he'd gone underground, back to this Yorktown neighborhood where he once strangled his associate's girlfriend because she mocked his exceptionally small feet. If he's in New York, where? Big Frank would never harbor. Gina, though. Yes. Where? The Royal York itself? Then that strange murder of her coworker.

He requisitions the real estate records for all Royal York condos. All 494. Who lives in each condo. Who owns each condo. Gina R owned a condo on the 9th floor facing south and a 13th floor one-bedroom facing north, with a view of the interior garden. The 13th floor condo was unoccupied and had been so for 5 years exactly, since it was purchased in her name by her father. Did the 13th floor condo have an intermittent visitor? Does it have one now? Where the black dog is kept, who did not show himself at the 9th floor condo when Angel delivered the dog food, who never barked when Angel entered because Blackie was not there? Because he was in the 13th floor condo, with Jimmy? He tells himself to restrain his excitement.

* * *

She presents him the following morning at 7 a.m. with the promised toothbrush and a new tube of toothpaste. He'd been awake unbeknownst to her at 3 a.m., when he'd crawled delicately out of her bed to work his phone in the living room: to access the special apps that he'd used routinely in his job. He was in search of a name, through various data bases—a residence, a criminal record, if it existed, of one Charles Gasko. There were two: one deceased, 1934, in Pickaway Ohio, another the owner of a fictitious Facebook account, who described himself as editor-in-chief and publisher of an avant-garde press specializing in aviary porn and vegetarian cook books, located in American Samoa.

No living Charles Gasko in the United States.

10

A lingering embrace, a long kiss, and Mike Garcia says good-bye to Gina Rendonello and begins to drive back down to the 7th Precinct Station on the FDR—it's rush hour and abnormally uncongested. The few cars on the road fly by him at crazily high speeds. He's not driven more than 5 minutes when he takes an exit to a quiet street—and parks. To think. To put together what much later, as he and Ventura faced a gaggle of swarming reporters, what Garcia would call a "grand theory," but what Ventura would say was the "miraculous" intervention of St. Jude, to which a twenty-something reporter for the *New York Times* (a Protestant) said, Who's that? Saint who?

At his desk on Pitt he dials the 17th, identifies himself, says this is urgent, very, he needs to speak with Vince Ventura. He tells Ventura that he's the lead in the Kidd murder. Ventura says, I appreciate, but that's your territory. You think I can help? Garcia reviews the events of the previous day—including, with awkwardness, the night he spent with Gina. He describes the encounter in the lobby. He recounts the details of the tracking of the ghostly runner from the Williamsburg Bridge to The Royal York. The guy tracked by the civic-minded African-Americans, Detective Ventura, is the guy who stepped off the elevator with a big black dog. The description fits. The outfit. The partial baldness. If he's not Kidd's killer, I'm not a Spic. Vince says, Amazing, Mike. I'm happy for you. You likely got your man. He had a big black dog on a leash? You connect Gina strongly, you're guessing—it's only a guess—that she knows the man holding the leash? Mike says,

So you're thinking what I'm thinking? Vince says, Even though you can't say it, much less me, you have Kidd's killer in the net and you also—I'm thinking, I'm imagining out of my mind—you also have something else you reeled in by the luck which I never had. You hooked Jimmy Rendonello. Mike says, Possibly. Vince says, Two fish with one hook. Possibly? I say, I pray, definitely.

Vince informs Mike about Gina's two condos. He says, I believe Gina is harboring her uncle. She's going down for that, assuming that guy with the dog is Jimmy. Mike says, Okay, not *possibly* the uncle. It *is* the uncle, she's harboring, but I'm also pretty confident she hasn't the foggiest idea that Jimmy, the uncle, Jimmy—it was Jimmy who killed Kidd, unless she egged him on by talking about Kidd's behavior—not encouraging him directly, but in an innocent way—and Vince cuts in with, Which in a way is more horrible, she'll have to live with that—the innocent egging on of the homicidal maniac who cuts out Kidd's tongue. No, Mike says, she never openly encouraged that, I spent time with her and—Vince cuts in, You have a thing for her, your judgment might be naïve, let's factor in your thing for her. It's possibly in the family blood, though I have a hard time going to that length of interpretation. Mike says, Is it for sure Jimmy? Whoever the guy really is, I make him for Kidd, but the guy is not necessarily Jimmy. Vince says, You're right. Not necessarily. But he is.

* * *

Ventura and Garcia drive to The Royal York in Garcia's car. They review the details of the plan. They go into the lobby after showing their badges to the doorman and speak to the concierge, identify themselves again, tell her they need to check something in the garage. Two specific parking spaces. In complete confidence, they tell her. If Gina Rendonello is alerted by you there's a serious charge attached to your betrayal of law enforcement agents, which is not nice for you, Linda. The concierge gives them the numbers which are not, for security reasons, identical with condo numbers. The numbers of the spaces which they've requested belong to Gina. No vehicle is parked in Gina's space, as was expected. Vince had determined that she didn't own a car. There is one parked in the space reserved for a Charles Gasko, as Linda had informed them.

They each run a database for California residents only, a more granular base than the FBI's, which is for the entire country. They learn that there is no Charles Gasko in California, who yet somehow owns this California-plated Audi A-8, registered in his name. Mike says, False I.D. documents gets him past regulations. He gets driver's license. Buys car. Now what, Vince?

The garage is of course dimly lit. They hear footsteps, as in a conventional thriller movie, and quickly retreat to the street and Mike's vehicle—convinced that Charles Gasko is Jimmy Rendonello, the killer of Jon Kidd. They have him, here at The Royal York. He's in the 13th Floor condo, because his car is parked. Or out walking the dog? Or running the East River trail? Or visiting Gina, at her condo? Or she's visiting him in his? Or something ordinary that people do? They stepped out for lunch.

You have something going with her, am I right? Vince says. You're not wrong, Vince. Obviously, Vince says, you have her cell number. Call her. She picks up, you say I miss you madly. Can I come up? I'm in pain. I need to make love with you again. Can't wait. Etcetera. See what happens, Mike. So Mike calls. She picks up. How sweet, she says, but I'm going to need some time to think us over—so fast, I'm really drawn to you, but we, for sure I, need a little space before we make another—What? he says. Another what? Leap, she says. Into your bed, Gina. They laugh. They agree to talk tomorrow. Genuine romantic hesitation—or is Uncle Jimmy with her? Now what?

They return to the lobby and ask the concierge to ring the occupant of the 13th floor condo in question. No answer. They ask her to ring Gina. She does. If she picks up, say, Sorry, I dialed the wrong number. No answer. Now what, Vince, I defer to you? We go to Gina's, expecting and prepared. You're carrying, I'm carrying. But before we do that, we go back to his car and fuck it up. Flat tire? Worse, Vince says. Worse, how? says Mike. Vince grins as he takes from his sport coat a tracking device.

Finalities

Jimmy

But not with a bang: Because Linda the concierge knew a thing
or two and refused to give Ventura and Garcia a master key. If
you want to enter those condos—bust in, to be blunt—you need
a no-knock search warrant. Which would take, they knew, a few
hours, at best. Foiled in their intention to storm, if necessary, the
condos in question, they sit in the lobby at a loss. After 15 minutes
marked with an expletive quietly voiced, they step outside pac-
ing (shit), assuring each other (shit) that one way or another they
had Jimmy. The tracking device (but should he switch vehicles?)
would guarantee his capture and incarceration for life. They had
him, though not quite. And then they had him.

There they are, Jimmy and Gina, here they come rounding
the corner at 64th and York, bearing down on The Royal York.
They've been running the East River Trail. Here they come chat-
ting, Jimmy laughing, as Ventura and Garcia step forward, guns
drawn. Jimmy stops, says, Hey! Don't Forget! Blackie needs to be
walked! May I introduce you to my fabulous niece, the one and
only Gina? You, he says, pointing at Garcia—you and Gina, think
I don't know? Treat her right. My succulent goose is cooked. Puts
his wrists together, underside to underside, saying Cuff me, Dano.
Which of you will take care of Blackie? Garcia, lowering his .38,
says I will.

Vince Ventura is deflated. He's defeated. Because for 16
years he imagined a dramatic face-off—good guy from the Bronx
vs. bad guy from the Bronx. He could never imagine that Red
Rendonello would fail to stay in character.

Jimmy says, Hey! Garcia! In case you're wondering. Beautiful
Blackie here gobbled up that asshole's tasty tongue.

Jimmy says, I shit even on shit itself.

Marie Rose

Radiological testing showed aggressive cancer. The surgery was scheduled soon after the five boroughs were locked down. What will be removed, she told Vince, in my radical hysterectomy, is the entire uterus, tissue on the sides of the uterus, my cervix, and the top part of my vagina. Our vagina. When she finished telling Vince, he collapsed. When he came to, she said, There's a silver lining. After 8 weeks, we resume our sex life. He says nothing. She says, I am told it will be normal again. He says nothing. She says, Here's another silver lining, more silver: They say chances are very good our sex life will be hotter than before. Can you handle that? Can I?

Akash

Akash, Akash, where are you?

In lockdown, no privilege is accorded to The Yale Club of New York City. It must close its elite door. The waiters, the supervisory personnel staff, the doormen, the luggage room staff, the kitchen staff, the maids, the front desk staff, the Lounge staff, the Library staff, the gym staff, the information operators and other workers never seen are furloughed—do not say "fired" or "let go"—to go home and apply for unemployment benefits. These men and women who had lived paycheck to paycheck were awarded—while employed—a significant piece of the 18% service charge added to all Club guests' bills. In addition to hourly salary. Year after year virtually no turn over—satisfaction written on their faces. And the guests were invariably appreciative as they slipped them supplemental tips, a crisp 20, sometimes more. So they waited, all the furloughed waited for the end of lockdown, when their world would return, as in the good time before.

The parents of Jade Miranda called the Club to ask for Akash's contact information. The Club shared his cell and physical address. They called. Not in service. They wrote. Return to sender. Address unknown.

Crisis

When the order for Lockdown was announced, the Club gave guests 3 days to depart. Antonio Robinson made a decision. He had a choice—Eliot Conte did not. On Eliot Conte's behalf a choice was made.

Arthur Avenue

Times metro reporter #1 to *Times* metro reporter #2: How many businesses that've been around in this town forever—from what I hear they might go belly up in this lockdown. Reporter #2: Too many, but maybe not in the Bronx. Reporter #1: Hell hole of poverty, minorities, violent crimes. Reporter #2 (in his mid-60s): How old are you? Twenty-eight, am I right? Ever heard of, ever visited Arthur Avenue? Go up there. A new arrow in your little quiver.

On Arthur Avenue, near 187th Street, she interviews a man about her age as he's sitting on a bench outside a shuttered restaurant. He tells her he's the son of the owner. She says, Does your father—he says, My mother. She says, Sorry for the sexist assumption. Does she, your mother, think she'll open again? Like ever? The young guy says, You're not Italian, am I right? No, I'm not, she says. What's your ethnic background? She says, My great grandparents were Polish, I think. He says, You *think*? Not that different from Italians, know what I mean? She says, Oh. Right. I guess. He says, That restaurant across the street, Rigoletto's? Dominic's down the street, where you don't order, they lay it on the table what they have? At the end they give you the check, just the amount, no itemizing of what you ate. God forbid you should ask. You kidding me? The classic stores—Egidio's? DeLillo's? Casa della Mozzarella? Madonia Bakery? Calabria Pork Store? Opening again? Does the bear etcetera in the woods? Know those massive trees they have in California? I forget the name. She says, Redwoods? Yeah. We can't be moved. Italians are Redwoods. We don't acknowledge change, forget outside influence. That's my answer to you, sweetheart. Arthur Avenue goes back to the same. On Arthur Avenue, the virus loses. Feel free to take off that mask and quote me accurately.

Ventilator

Jade Miranda was at last taken off her ventilator and wheeled smoothly to the hospital's overwhelmed morgue.

Blackie

As they stared frozen at drawn guns she did not speak. What could she have said? Not to Ventura, a face unknown, but to Mike Garcia, to whom the previous afternoon, evening, and night she had relinquished herself to a sliver of hope for a less lonely future. He's a phony, nothing more, he betrayed me to bring down my dear uncle. My dear deadly Uncle Jimmy. She never denied it, deadly, whom she had loved for all those years while bearing her dark knowledge. Uncle Jimmy, whose abiding concern was not for himself, or her, but for the gentle big black dog.

Garcia and Ventura would take Jimmy to be arraigned. Blackie would go home with Mike. To become his and everyone's best friend. This dog. Because any dog is to be embraced over most humans. What'll she do? He left a message on her phone to say that "we are absolutely real together," but adding that he could not look the other way when… he could not complete the thought. She did not return the call.

He promised her in another unanswered call that she would not face a charge of knowingly harboring a fugitive. He would cover for her "somehow." "Somehow," she would write to him after the trial that would find her guilty and send her away for 18 months, to be released after 10 in consideration of exemplary behavior.

Her father, Big Frank himself (which is how he was always referred to in print and conversation: Big Frank himself) did not survive his proximity to brother Jimmy and rumors about Jimmy's escape 16 years prior, that he'd been in periodic contact with Jimmy all the while. There was no evidence for Big Frank's complicity, but Delta required no evidence. They fired him without cause. His daughter would only find occasional work piloting the sleek small jets of the very rich.

Garcia tried repeatedly after her release, but she would not again relinquish. Not with you or anyone else.

Though convinced that Jimmy Rendonello had killed Jon Kidd, Garcia had nothing that would stand up in court. Rendonello was tried and convicted for the numerous murders he'd ordered and done himself long ago. Garcia had only a theory: that Jimmy had somehow lured Kidd out on East 10th because he intended to avenge his daughter (as he thought of her) for Kidd's abusive mouth (his tongue), that he did it quickly and coldly because he was an efficient psychopath.

And there is this to say: Gina was lost to him for good. For comfort and warmth, Mike Garcia had a theory—and a dog called Blackie.

Generosity

Though instrumental in the capture and conviction of Red Rendonello, at a nationally televised news conference Mike Garcia gave all credit to Vince Ventura, saying his own contribution was "only minor." When Vince said I could not have gotten to first base without this guy, Mike said, He's the man. He's totally the man. You don't see this kind of modesty these days. If book and movie deals come his way, which why wouldn't they, I can only say, I am honored to be mentioned in the same breath with Detective Ventura.

Marie Rose Ventura recovered well and speedily. They resumed their remarkable intimacy more intensely than before. Just like the first time, twice weekly.

To the Max

Rendonello was sentenced to life at a maximum security prison for the worst in West Virginia, where the guards took an early lunch two days after his arrival, giving a nod to a Mafia enforcer who, with a heavy lock wrapped in a sock, beat Jimmy to death in the head and face. He was dead after 1 minute, but the beating continued until where there was once a face there was now only a bowl of multi-colored oatmeal.

Melody

She showers. Deodorant. Makeup. Perfume. Washes, dries, and puts dishes away. Cleans sink, stove. Hands and knees, on floor pushing empty beer cans and fast food wrappers into 3 large trash bags. Collects newspapers, hands and knees: 6 large trash bags. Sweating profusely. Drags trash bags to rear hallway. On couch, wet, breathing hard. Floor again, hands and knees with towels, dusting. Prone on floor. Spent. Asleep. To shower. Deodorant. Makeup. Perfume. Turns on all lights. On couch. What now shall she do? Cell in hand. What shall she ever do? Cell vibrating. Caller ID: A Robinson.

Since They Were Kids

They would take long walks together, Conte and Robinson, through Utica's neighborhoods, beginning at age 9, when they would assist Conte's Italian-American political kingpin father by distributing election literature door-to-door in Utica's various wards. Thereafter they did it for themselves, for the feeling of friendship as they strolled talking about everything and nothing, for the pleasure of taking in the sections of town that looked nothing like their own East Side. The Polish West Side, the mixed ethnicities of the North and South Sides (the "mongrel" or "American" neighborhoods, as they were called), the densely and homogenous Italian East Side. A black boy and a white boy touring the unenlightened town where no ugly racist actions were undertaken—only words in thought and in private words among family members and in the quiet policies of the banks. Into and well beyond their young adult years they walked together until it became too painful for two men, several years ago, in their late 60s, physically assaulted by their bodies and in medical breakdown, to continue. And then they would sit on each other's front porches looking at, but not much registering the passing human traffic: not even the pretty girls. They sat quietly, without speaking, except for this occasional and typical snatch of dialogue:

—We got old.

—We didn't. They did. The bodies, the flesh.

—Notice how they say his *body* was found? Not he him*self*?

—Where did *he* go?

—Missing in Action

* * *

The Yale Club of New York City had given all guests and staff three days to evacuate. "Evacuate," they said, as if in a war zone. All gone except Conte and Robinson and Dmitri at the front desk. No doorman. It was the late afternoon of the third day.

Conte proposed one more walk together. Not far. Just up Vanderbilt a ways and then west to 5th Avenue and north along the Avenue, just a few blocks where Dmitri had informed him there was a bookstore. Unfortunately, B&N, Dmitri said. Plus truly bad coffee.

They made it to the top of Vanderbilt. Too hard. Back to the Club to take the elevator to the deserted and ill-lit Lounge. No drinks available. Where was Akash? Where was Jade?

Robinson asks Conte if he's been in touch with "the wife and the kid." Catherine and Annie. Conte said he had checked in with her a few times. Did you tell her about your conversations with the big shot producer? No. Going to tell her. No.

It's going to be difficult, Robby, to fly back to Syracuse. La Guardia to Atlanta. Atlanta to Las Vegas. Las Vegas to Toronto. Toronto to Buffalo. Buffalo to Syracuse. Endless layovers. Four days. Robinson says, That's no problem for me. So you'll do it? No. What are you going to do? I talked it over with Melody. I made her happy. I'm going to her place. To clean the apartment for her. Cook real stuff for her. I've decided, El. To make the move we didn't make back then, when we could've. You're joking. I'm moving in with her. Seriously? Yes.

El, we're on the downside, We're going down. But I still have wings. We're not done exploring. How about you? There's a train out of Grand Central. Take your suitcase across the street and make a reservation on the slow boat to China, which gets you back to Utica in 9 hours on a 200-mile run, but you get there, where you belong, with Catherine and Annie. You'll make that reservation, right? Leave tonight?

I'm turning myself in, Robby, or else it'll be worse for me. Three to five in prison. The producer brought charges for a verbal death threat. He's in bed with the Manhattan D.A. I'm turning myself over in a couple of hours. Pay the bail, El. Prisons are breeding grounds for this awful thing, this is what they're saying. You make bail, you get on the train. You disappear. Disappear, Robby? How disappear? NYPD detectives can't go Upstate? Do I want to be cuffed at home? In front of my family?

Whether here or in Utica, El, the family is devastated. Where are you taking my daddy? Why? When are you coming back, daddy? Because you could not control yourself and think about protecting Catherine and Annie from your selfish impulses, not that I'm a good example. You came here to protect her from the producer and her own ambition, which is ridiculous at this stage of her life, and what did you do? You end up destroying her and your daughter—and you destroy yourself. This thing? This virus? Over 65, like us? We're in the death zone. Jails breed this thing. You really want to die?

Conte: Hungry? For The Last Supper?

Robinson: Definitely.

Conte: Dining is closed here. Restaurants everywhere are in lockdown.

Robinson: We could go across the street to Grand Central. The lower level, the 42nd Street Oyster Bar. It's legendary.

Conte: I already asked Dmitri. It's shut down.

Robinson: What about all those fast food eateries on the lower level?

Conte: Dmitri says unlikely any are open and even if one is—

Robinson: Better to starve than to eat that garbage.

Conte: I'm not that hungry. You?

Robinson: Not that hungry... So what's your defense against this criminal charge? Christ, El, what can I do to get you out of this safe, home?

Conte does not respond. After a long silence, he's prodded by Robinson, who says, El? Your defense? He responds. He says: I have none... One more time, Robby? The weather's not bad today. Shall we try one more time to take one last walk?

In Italian, El. Say it in Italian.

Antonio, un'ultima passeggiata?

Acknowledgments

Jody McAuliffe
Jeff Jackson

About the Author

After ground-breaking work as a literary theorist, Frank Lentricchia changed his focus in the early 1990s and since has written a number of novels that explore ethnic and artistic identity within the context of contemporary American political disasters (Vietnam, Iraq) and in Manhattan Meltdown the global crisis of Covid-19. His books have been translated into Spanish, Japanese, Korean, Chinese, and Turkish. He was born to working-class parents in Utica, New York, first in the extended family to attend college. He lives in Durham, North Carolina, and was elected to the American Academy of Arts and Sciences in 2013.

Fiction By Frank Lentricchia

Manhattan Meltdown
The Glamour of Evil / A Place in the Dark
The Morelli Thing
The Dog Killer of Utica
The Accidental Pallbearer
The Portable Lentricchia
The Sadness of Antonioni
The Italian Actress
The Book of Ruth
Lucchesi and The Whale
The Music of the Inferno
The Knifemen
Johnny Critelli
The Edge of Night (faux memoir/fiction)